VisionSight

A Novel

Connie Lacy

Wild Falls Publishing
~~~
Atlanta, GA
~~~

ISBN-13: 978-0-9996084-3-2

Published by Wild Falls Publishing
PO Box 29452
Atlanta, GA 30359

*For my brown, green, hazel
and blue-eyed family*

~~~

Books by Connie Lacy

A Daffodil for Angie
The Time Telephone
VisionSight: a Novel
The Shade Ring, Book 1 of The Shade Ring Trilogy
Albedo Effect, Book 2 of The Shade RingTrilogy
Aerosol Sky, Book 3 of The Shade Ring Trilogy
Shade Ring Trilogy: Complete Trilogy Books 1 – 3
(ebook box set)
~~~

1.

It happened in the drive-through on my way to work. Just as I set my cup in the drink holder an odd sensation swept over me. It was like the aroma of coffee whispered a secret to the neurons in my brain that raced to my fingertips, causing them to tingle as I gripped the steering wheel. And I knew something momentous would happen that day. But I had no idea it would begin with a phone call from a number I didn't recognize. A phone call that would send a tremor through my life, changing it forever.

I'd always had strange premonitions. They weren't specific, though. It was more like a flash of intuition that something was just around the corner. But as I sipped my cappuccino, squinting into the morning sunshine streaming through my windshield, I had no clue whether I was about to win the lottery or run head-on into a MARTA bus.

The school day started routinely enough. Two students

absent. One who should've stayed home but didn't. Maria, my wonderful, bi-lingual teacher's aide, played her guitar and led the children in some songs as I took care of paperwork. Then we did our Fun with Math activity.

And just as I was getting the kids lined up for P.E. and helping Luis tie his shoe, my phone vibrated. Normally I would've let it roll over to voicemail but I thought it might be Alex. We'd only been dating a few weeks but there was no denying I was falling hard for him. I'd also auditioned for a part in a new play at the Midtown Theatre and had my fingers crossed for a callback. And, of course, I was already on alert for something out of the ordinary. But when I pulled the phone from my pocket I couldn't identify the number.

It was the hospital calling.

*

"Jenna, just do what you need to do," Maria whispered, brushing her long black hair out of her face. "I can handle the kids. Get going! It's your mother, for Christ's sake."

I realized one of the children was holding my hand. I looked down into Daisy's round face and brushed wisps of stringy blonde hair out of her eyes. She was my little sweetie and seemed to sense something was wrong.

"Miss Stevens?" she said.

I gave her hand a squeeze, gathered my things and stopped by the office on my way out.

As I drove, I debated whether to call Dad. My parents divorced when I was little but they were still friends. I decided to wait till I got to the hospital and had more information. The nurse had given me only the barest details. Heart attack on the elliptical machine at the Y. Ironic, my mom, the health nut, would have a heart attack while working out. She was the one always nagging everyone else to eat fruit and vegetables. And she definitely practiced what she preached as though her life depended on it.

When I passed the street where I grew up, I tried to remember my father being there with Mom and me. Only one memory came to mind. At least I think it was a memory and not a dream. I remembered the two of them sitting at the kitchen table and her saying "I just can't look into your eyes anymore." No yelling. No drama. Just those quiet words. And I thought what a weird thing for Mommy to say to Daddy. He has such warm, green eyes. I couldn't imagine anyone not wanting to look into those eyes. When Dad saw me in the doorway he picked me up and carried me back to bed where he sang me a song. A song about sunshine.

I thought about her as I drove. I loved my mother, but she was always busy with her career. She was a real estate agent, and a good one, I think. President of the Realtors Association and a board member with the Chamber of Commerce. Quite the businesswoman. But she'd always been so aloof – multi-tasking when she talked with me, making notes, typing a report, searching online. And our conversations were always direct and to the point. When I needed warmth or humor, I went to Dad's house.

I turned left at the steakhouse where we celebrated my

graduation from college. What an awkward evening. I was basking in everyone's attention and feeling pretty good since I'd already been hired to teach kindergarten at Cliffdale Elementary. They were making toasts in my honor. But Mom was working on her third margarita, and with each one, her voice got a little louder and her eyes a little more glazed. Then she stood up, held her glass high and cleared her throat.

"All right, people. It's my turn." And she looked in my general direction, but I had the feeling she was looking at my hair, not my face. "Okay, Jenna, here goes. May the wind always be at your back, may your glass be ever full, and may you always have clear vision as you look to the future." And she cackled like she'd just told a side-splitting inside joke.

But as the others raised their glasses, Mom turned hers up, drained it and plopped down again in her chair, embarrassing my grandparents almost as much as me.

"Is that an Irish toast?" Dad asked.

"Well, they don't call me Anne Kelly for nothing," she said and waved our waiter over to order another drink.

*

I pushed "5" after getting directions to the ICU and watched the elevator doors close. They were those mirrored doors that forced you to look at your reflection. I combed my hair with my fingers, smoothing out the tousles. People said I resembled my mother when she was young. The same golden brown hair, same height – five six. But my eyes were green, like Dad's, not hazel like

Mom's. I liked to think my personality was more like his too. I checked my outfit just before the doors opened. Grey slacks, white blouse, blue jacket. Professional looking. Mom would approve.

She was hooked up to a collection of tubes and wires. There were instruments beeping quietly beside her bed. I stood for a moment, adjusting to the environment, like letting your eyes get used to the dark. Her chest was rising and falling so I knew she was breathing.

Then a doctor in blue scrubs appeared. He was a tall, middle-aged man with a surgical mask hanging from his neck as though he'd just come from surgery.

"Any change?" he asked the nurse trailing behind him.

"No change," she said, checking a monitor by the bed.

"I'm Dr. Knox," he said, shaking my hand and nodding. "You're the daughter?"

"Yes."

"I'm not going to beat around the bush. Your mother's had a major heart attack but we're doing everything we can."

"Is she going to…" I said, but my voice caught in my throat.

"Well, I don't have a crystal ball but you need to prepare yourself for the worst. Do you have any relatives you can call?"

"My dad," I whispered.

He nodded.

"Any questions?" he said.

He waited a few seconds but when I didn't reply, he

bustled from the room, the nurse following him as though she was attached to him by an invisible cord.

I approached the bed, looking down at my mother's pale face. Her hair, always styled just so, was now plastered to her head. She had no lipstick or makeup on, which looked so unnatural. She was only 52 but suddenly looked much older. I thought about holding her hand but just stood there. That's when I saw her eyelids flutter. She opened her eyes for a second before closing them again. A moment later she opened them once more. She turned her head so she could see me better and swallowed, fixing her gaze on my mouth. She said something but it was too muffled for me to make out the words.

"I'm here, Mom," I said, keeping my voice low.

I reached for her hand. Her grip was weak.

"Jenna," she whispered.

I leaned closer, straining to hear.

"Important," she said, her eyes shut tight like she was in pain. "Sight."

"What?"

"Vision."

She gripped my hand more tightly.

"In my room," she said.

I was trying to figure out what she was talking about when she pulled me closer and grasped both of my hands in hers. Then she breathed deeply, and as she let out her breath, she stared into my eyes. I felt a hot current travel through my hands, up my arms and through my body. My eyes were locked onto hers – I couldn't look away. It was as though I was witnessing scenes from long ago – events from her life. Like watching a herky-jerky movie, disjointed episodes fast-forwarding from one to the next. I saw her rushing into the emergency room and finding her mother holding her father's limp hand, and bursting into tears when she realized he was dead. Then she was with a handsome young man – yes, my father – and kissing him. Next, I saw her giving birth. The baby was me. Then she was looking into her own mother's eyes, a frightened expression on her face, as her mother died. Finally, I watched as she held onto a bar, obviously in excruciating pain, and then there was blackness. I gasped as the terrifying scenes passed before me.

At last I could see the hospital room again. I was still holding her hands in mine, but now they were limp. And although her eyes were still open, it was obvious they could no longer see. My mother was dead.

2.

Naturally, my dad was out of the country. He was an epidemiologist with the CDC and they sometimes sent him to the ends of the earth to do research or help out when there was a disease outbreak. This time, he was in Africa. I called and left a message about Mom, telling him I was okay because I knew he couldn't just pack up and fly home. But to tell the truth, I was shaken. It was like I'd lived through an earthquake so violent that it rearranged the furniture of my mind, jostling connections and altering electrical activity.

My brain couldn't wrap itself around my mother's death. She was always in control. How could she let herself die like that? Of course, that was just the kind of thing Mom would say. Like when she accused a salesman at her company of coming down with a cold because he didn't wash his hands enough and didn't eat healthy. Or when she judged that the receptionist "wouldn't have arthritis in her knees if she'd lose some of that weight." No allowance for luck or genes. It was inconceivable that my mother, of all people, would die of a heart attack.

If I'd had a clue what fate held in store, maybe I would've tried to be closer with her. I don't know. The more I thought about it though, the less plausible it seemed. Mom was just so... distant.

But maybe she'd reached out to me there at the end. I was still reeling from those final moments. It was such an eerie, terrifying experience – her life flashing before my eyes. What the hell was that all about? Was it my imagination? A hallucination? It was like our minds had been linked for a moment. I didn't understand it.

It was nearly noon when I trudged up the stairs and unlocked the door of my apartment. Thankfully, Tia wouldn't be home from work till after three. While she was my best friend and roommate, I wasn't ready to face anyone. Talking would take way too much strength.

I turned off my phone, locked my bedroom door, lowered the shades and lay on my bed. I studied the room for a moment – the room I'd been so proud of when we moved in two years ago. It was all white and yellow, like you'd see in a decorating magazine, and I suddenly wished it were dark blue. I closed my eyes and took a slow, deep breath, trying to relax my body.

Then I was peering into a pair of grey eyes where I could see giant waves topped by foamy whitecaps. I was in a boat being tossed on rough seas and there was pounding, pounding, as though the hull of the ship was about to splinter. I knew there was no way out of this storm. The ship would sink with me on it. There was no one to save me and I couldn't save myself. I sat straight up in bed, a scream stuck in my throat. But the only sound was gurgling as I struggled for air, holding my hands to my face, knowing full well they were my mother's eyes.

And I realized Tia was knocking on my door.

"Jenna, you all right?"

I let her in and sat down on my bed, staring at the floor.

"Your dad called and said he couldn't reach you and he was worried and I was worried and when I got here your door was locked and I was, like, scared, you know?"

I rubbed my temples.

"Your dad says he's leaving his phone on and you should call him right away. He's, like, bordering on frantic."

I nodded my head without looking at her, and lay down again, lacking the energy for anything more.

"Jenna," she said, more quietly now. "I'm so sorry about your mom. Is there anything I can do?

I shook my head.

She walked to the side of the bed. I opened my eyes and looked up at her. She was fidgeting, examining her long fingernails. We'd been friends since elementary school, but now I was reminded how truly striking she was. She was the quintessential beautiful black woman – large, almond-shaped brown eyes, perfect skin, her hair done in short, soft ringlets. She was tall and slender and looked like she belonged on the cover of *Elle* or *Essence,* not teaching a class of second graders. When she realized I'd opened my eyes, she met my gaze.

The breath was knocked out of me as I was seized by a series of images – once again like a movie fast-forwarding at great speed. First I saw Tia drunk at a party; then having sex with my boyfriend, Alex; I saw her hiding liquor bottles behind a shoe rack in her closet; then I saw her looking heavier and older sitting at a bar with a strange man. The next scene was Tia holding a tiny baby in her arms in a hospital room. And then there was a horrifying scene where she stumbled drunk into the kitchen, put a frying pan on the stove, poured oil in the pan, lit the burner and then wandered into the living room and passed out on the couch. I could see flames and smoke and knew that Tia, and whoever else was in that house, would not survive. And then my vision went dark and I was released.

My hands covered my face. It was like I was losing my mind – suffering psychotic delusions. My body felt like I'd just lifted a car, my head was throbbing and I was breathing hard.

"Jenna, what's wrong? Are you sick? Can you hear me?"

Afraid to open my eyes, I just held my hand up, trying to get her to stop talking. I didn't know how to answer. I was not all right. Why was I having these waking nightmares? Was this what it was like taking a psychedelic drug? Had I accidentally ingested something without my knowledge?

The doorbell rang and she disappeared. Then I heard Alex's voice in the living room.

The exertion of getting up to lock my door left me dizzy. But there was no way I was letting her bring Alex in my room. I remembered the vision of the two of them in bed together. I think it was her bedroom here at our apartment. The sheets were pink, like hers. It was all too disturbing.

"Jenna?" she called through the door. "Alex is here."

"Not now."

I shuffled into my bathroom and washed my face. I had to clear my head. Had to figure out what was going on. I thought back to what happened in the hospital room as I splashed my face with water. The craziness began when Mom held my hands in hers and looked in my eyes. What was it she said? Something about vision. I thought she was incoherent, just babbling nonsense. But she told me to look in her room.

*

The weeping willow swayed in the breeze as I pulled into the driveway, as though in mournful greeting. I helped Mom plant it when I was five, shortly after the divorce.

A lamp was on in the living room when I walked through the front door. I punched the code, turning off the security system, and looked around. You would've thought the house was on the market – it was immaculate. No dust, nothing out of place. You could drop in on my mother any time, day or night, and find everything in perfect order. She had a maid who came by once a week, but Mom was just a neatnik, bordering on obsessive-compulsive.

The living room was decorated in greens and blues, with paintings on the walls that she found at local art galleries. In fact, the whole house was done in various shades of green and blue, making me feel like I was standing on the bank of a secluded pond, surrounded by thick forest.

She'd always been proud that she lived in historic Decatur, which she thought was more prestigious than an Atlanta address, although in most people's minds, it was just a suburb of the larger city.

I mounted the stairs, heading for her bedroom, which was spotless like the rest of the house. But the room smelled like Mom – like the slightly fruity cologne she always wore – making me feel like I was invading her privacy. The queen size bed was covered with a pale blue duvet, a sea-foam green bed skirt peeking out below. A small bedside lamp gave a soft glow to the room, but I turned on the overhead light as well.

What was I looking for? A diary maybe? I scanned the room, wondering where to start. The mahogany dresser and chest of drawers gleamed in the light – they were obviously polished every week. Mom's large jewelry box sat atop the dresser. She never wore expensive jewelry but was careful to wear tasteful jewelry with all her business suits and outfits.

Beginning with the top drawer of the chest, I rummaged through the contents. Her underwear and clothing were arranged with great care. There was nothing in the chest, so I moved on to the dresser. There were scarves, sweaters, stockings – all the things you'd expect, but no diary.

Opening the closet, I surveyed her wardrobe and shoes. Lots of greens and blues. I realized then that her house and her closet were devoid of warmth. She surrounded herself, and even dressed herself, in cool colors. Funny, how I'd never noticed that before. At least, not consciously.

Where would she keep a diary if she had one? I opened the drawers of the nightstands on either side of the bed. Expensive note cards, several pens, two small alarm clocks, a pair of reading glasses and two full-color gardening books along with several Jane Austen novels.

I glanced around the room. Was there anything to find?

On the dresser, there was a triptych frame with photos of me in it – one when I was a baby, one when I was about five, and my high school graduation picture. There was another framed photo of me, Dad and the Australian Shepherd I had when I was a kid. Funny that Mom would have that picture on her dresser. I strolled over and picked it up to look more closely.

My grandmother – my dad's mother – snapped the photo the summer I was 10. Fourth of July picnic at Grandma and Grandpa's lake house, red and white checked tablecloth on the picnic table, the lake in the background. Me scratching Boomer's ears, Dad rubbing my head like I was a dog too. Big smiles. Why would Mom have a picture of her ex-husband on her dresser?

I whirled around, wondering where her photo albums were. The closet. Yes, I'd seen them. I opened the closet again and pulled four albums from a side shelf. The first one had recent pictures in it. Lots of photos of me. The second one was filled with pictures from when I was a child. The third album included pictures from before I was born. Pictures I'd never seen. Photos of Mom and Dad smiling in front of the Eiffel Tower. One where Mom was sitting on Dad's lap, mugging for the camera. Holding hands on the beach. They looked so much in love. What the hell happened?

I opened the next one – the one with pictures of me as a baby and toddler. We looked like such a happy family then. The little blonde girl and her doting parents. And then I turned the page and there was a picture of Nana's grave marker. Mom's mother died when I was four. And that's where I found a yellowed envelope with my name on it. Inside was a letter from my mother.

3.

"Dearest Jenna," the letter began. I sat down on the bed. "First, let me say I'm sorry I'm not a better mother. I love you dearly and wish I could show it more. When you were very small I was able to do that. But my mother's death ruined my life, although I don't blame Mother.

"A few days before she died my mother revealed to me that she had inherited a gift from her mother. She called it 'the visionsight.' But I strongly disagree with her characterization. It's a curse, not a gift.

"She explained to me that I would be able to see some people's futures, and even their pasts, when I looked into their eyes. But only the people I care about, not strangers or casual acquaintances. And when she died, it was like a switch was flipped somewhere. I suddenly had this ability, even though I didn't want it. Why it works like that, I don't know. I wish there were some way I could avoid passing it along to you. But as you were growing up, it was obvious to me that you would inherit it when I die.

"So I have tried to be as healthy as I can, hoping to avoid burdening you for as long as possible. But I can't see my own future, although I've seen other people's. Unfortunately, it's a painful experience knowing ahead of time what's in the cards.

"It seems like you should be able to use this gift to make the world a better place, or at least to make people's lives better. But I haven't been able to figure out how to do that, no matter how many times I tried. I've never been able to prevent a tragedy, even if I've seen it beforehand. I don't believe my mother was able to do so either. I think she knew my father would die in a car wreck and was tormented by not being able to save him. So I don't have any sage advice on that score.

"What I've done is avoid looking into the eyes of the people I love because it's traumatic seeing bad things happen that I can't prevent.

"I'm sorry you'll have to carry this millstone around your neck someday. But I do have one suggestion, and that is to throw yourself into some kind of creative outlet – something you enjoy. I have my real estate career and my garden, which I love. I'm sure you'll also have activities that will be enjoyable and meaningful to you.

"My mother told me not to tell anyone about this. I can only imagine what would happen if word got out that we could see the future.

"Know that I love you.

"Mom"

I set the letter on the bed and rubbed my forehead, trying to make sense of it all.

Visionsight. That's what she said in the hospital. So, it wasn't that she passed it to me there in the ICU. I would've "inherited" it even if I hadn't been with her, I guess. It's just that when she died, it passed to me, and I just happened to be looking into her eyes as she breathed her last breath. And in that split second, I had my first visionsight. It was her life I saw. I wondered if she'd seen my life too when our eyes met.

And that memory from my childhood – Mom telling Dad "I just can't look into your eyes anymore" – came back to me. Now I knew why. She saw his future and must not have liked what she saw.

I stared at the neat handwriting and wondered when she wrote the letter. There was no date on it. Did she plan on talking with me, not realizing she had so little time? A letter seemed so impersonal.

The chiming of the doorbell brought my train of thought to a screeching halt. It had gotten dark out. Maybe a neighbor was at the door?

It was Meg. Of course. Dad sent her to check on me.

Avoiding her eyes was tricky. I didn't know how close you had to be with somebody to have that distressing vision thing, but I didn't want to tempt fate. I was very fond of Meg. She was more like a friend than a stepmother. She was fun to be with, clever and pretty, with intelligent, mischievous brown eyes and short brown hair. I always thought she and Dad were a good match, ever since they started dating during my junior year of high school. They reminded me of a pair of fluffy-tailed squirrels, chasing each other up and down a tree trunk just for the fun of it.

"Your dad called and told me about your mother. He's beside himself with worry."

It was awkward standing there with the door open, staring at her baby blue sweat suit. So I stepped back and motioned for her to come in. She immediately wrapped her arms around me.

"I'm so sorry," she said softly.

"Thanks."

"Why don't you spend the night at our house? I finished fixing up the guest room. Just got a new bedspread last week."

I backed into the living room, putting a little distance between us.

"Tom's trying to get a ticket to fly home," she said, "but it might take a couple of days. Can I help you with any of the arrangements?"

"Arrangements? Oh, right – funeral arrangements."

She stopped staring at me and looked around the room as though giving me a minute to steady myself.

"Your mother had very good taste in art," she said, studying an abstract painting on the wall that looked rather like air bubbles in deep water.

And I guess it was because I was avoiding looking at her face that I suddenly noticed she'd gained weight. But I realized the weight gain was only in her belly. It threw me for a loop when I realized what that meant and when she turned toward me again, I stared directly into her eyes.

The vision hit me like a rough wave on the beach when a hurricane is heading up the coast. I staggered backwards, sitting hard on the couch. I saw Meg giving birth to a baby boy, my dad crying tears of joy; then happy scenes in the house and yard with the three of them; then Meg standing solemnly next to Dad's hospital bed where he was hooked up to an IV, his eyes closed; and then an image of her standing in the cemetery crying over his grave, holding her little boy's hand. Good God! I covered my face and wept, overwhelmed by this wretched vision of their future.

Finally, I realized Meg was sitting next to me, her hand on my arm.

"I'm so sorry, Jenna. I shouldn't have said anything about the funeral."

I let her think that's what upset me as I tried to pull myself together. I was sick of this visionsight bullshit, or whatever it was. And this was just the first day of the rest of my life! How did my mother stand it? All those times I thought she was so aloof came flooding back to me. She didn't look directly at me because she didn't want to know what terrible things lay in wait. Like this nightmare I was living through right now!

*

When I got back to my apartment Tia and Alex were talking and having drinks in the living room. It was obvious they were waiting for me. I nodded as I hurried past them.

"Sorry, guys," I said. "I appreciate your concern but I'm

totally exhausted."

And I kept walking.

"Jenna!" Tia called, trailing after me.

"I'm going to bed."

"Alex just wants to…"

"I can't," I whispered.

I ducked into my room. Just before turning off my lamp I checked my phone and found two emails – one from my dad telling me to call him and one from Midtown Theatre asking me to come in for a callback audition the next day. It's what I'd been dreaming of. What a dreadful case of rotten timing.

4.

Breakfast was half a banana. I sat at the tiny pink Formica table Tia had bought online, sipping my coffee, trying to clear my head. They knew I wasn't coming to school today. A substitute would help Maria get through the day. And my audition wasn't until four.

I'd had bit parts at several local theaters but this was my first callback for a substantial role. In fact, it might be my big break. Don't get me wrong, I enjoyed teaching, but the plan had always been to get a degree in something so I could support myself while I pursued acting. Of course, I tried not to get my hopes up too much about all that.

Still, I wondered if I was doing the right thing. I'd agreed to be there for the callback, but doing it the day after my mother's death made me feel like I was tailgating on a freshly dug grave. Still, would Mom want me to miss such a big opportunity? One thing about it – I didn't know anyone at the theater well enough to have one of those damn visions. Which would be such a relief.

So maybe that's what I should do – avoid being around people I cared for: Dad, Meg, Tia, Alex. Of course, I cared for my students too. God, how could I go back and look in Daisy's eyes? What would I see there? I didn't want to know. Especially if there was nothing I could do about it. I'd have to learn the tricks my mom knew so well – never looking people in the eye unless I didn't give a hoot about them. The school year would be over in three weeks. If I could just hang in there that long. Bereavement leave would give me one week off. Then, I'd only have two weeks left in the classroom. I could practice not looking directly at the children.

*

At 3:45 I was pacing the burgundy carpet of the theater lobby. A blonde woman sat in a chair, studying her lines, mouthing them over and over to herself. She was dressed in jeans and a white top, which I thought was a mistake if she was trying out for the same part I was. I'd dressed in the outfit I'd worn to the first audition – a retro fifties dress with a full skirt and belted waist. It was pink with white accents and I was wearing white high heels. My lips were painted red and my hair was done in a French twist. A string of faux pearls and matching small earrings completed the look. The part they'd called me back for was the younger version of one of the lead characters in *Rose and Lily*, about two half-senile sisters.

Then it was my turn and I was ushered through the theater to the stage. The house lights were up so I could see a small cluster of people sitting near the front. The burgundy carpet of the lobby extended down the aisles, and the seats matched as well. A 1950s looking guy stood center stage, clearly a little bored, like maybe this was the umpteenth time he'd run the lines. Mid-thirties, about six feet tall, trim, dishwater blonde hair jelled into an early Elvis style.

He nodded as I joined him.

"Randall Hayes," he said.

"Jenna Stevens," I replied, trying for a friendly smile.

Bracing myself for the worst, I glanced briefly at his eyes and was tremendously relieved when nothing happened.

Of course, now that we were face to face, I realized who he was – one of a handful of actors who got most of the lead roles in local theater productions. And I knew why too. He was the son of an Atlanta developer whose philanthropy helped keep many local arts organizations solvent. It was expected he would get the roles he wanted. And he did.

Sam Novak, the director, was sitting in the third row with a couple of other people.

"So, uh… Jenna," he called out.

I'd met him at the first audition. Young, but his glasses gave him an authoritative air. He looked almost foreign. Dark hair, blue eyes, five ten maybe. Attractive, but not Hollywood handsome. He was – how should I put it – asymmetrical.

"You ready?" he called.

I nodded, pivoting away from Randall for a moment and then whirling around again.

"What do you mean you don't like being a father? It's a little late for that!" I said, giving him an angry look.

"Look, Rose," Randall said, sighing with realistic exasperation, "you're the one who wanted kids. Not me."

"We made that decision together. I certainly didn't ambush you," I said, seething.

"I didn't say you..."

"But you implied..."

"Listen, babe," he said, "I'm a good provider. That's my job and I do it well. Your job is to raise the kids. I mete out the punishment now and then, but you're the one who wanted children."

And before I knew what I was doing, my hand slapped his face.

"Hey!" he cried, touching his cheek.

"I'm sorry," I said, dropping out of character. "I don't know what came over me."

And then someone applauded, and I looked up to see the young director nodding his head and clapping slowly.

"Do me a favor," Sam called out, looking down at a notebook on his lap, "wait for me in the lobby, uh... Jenna. I'll be done in, say, fifteen minutes."

Thirty minutes later, my presumed rival hurried back through the lobby, looking like she was trying not to cry. Fifteen minutes after that, Sam moseyed toward me, pulling a sport coat on over his tee shirt and jeans. He tucked his horn-rimmed glasses in his pocket and motioned with his head for me to walk with him and we strolled down the street to a coffee shop. He ordered a black coffee and I got hot tea.

"Just wanted to get a feel for where you're coming from," he said once we were seated.

He looked younger without the glasses, making me wonder how he got this directing gig.

"Where I'm coming from?"

"Yeah."

I wasn't sure what he wanted to know.

"Why'd you slap his face?"

"He deserved it."

"So, you were rewriting the script?"

I sipped my tea, trying to figure out what to say. If he wasn't interested, he wouldn't be talking with me. But I didn't want to scare him off being... whatever might scare him off. So I shrugged. Then he shrugged and raised his eyebrow.

"Okay, Rose."

I swallowed and opened my mouth but nothing came out.

"Yeah, you got the part," he said.

Elated. Depressed. How could I be both at the same time? But that pretty much summed up my state of mind. Who could I share the news with? Two days before, I would've called Dad, Tia, Alex... and Mom. Not anymore.

*

Because my mother was such an organized person, arrangements had already been made for her cremation. So five days after she died, a box containing her ashes was delivered to my apartment by Federal Express. Dad said he'd help me plan a memorial service when he got back but who would come? She kept her distance from everyone and now I knew why. In retrospect, it seemed like she tried her best to find fault with people to make sure affection didn't sneak up on her.

And then her lawyer called to tell me she'd left everything to me – the house, which was paid for, a savings account, some investments, and the proceeds from her life insurance policy. It hadn't even occurred to me.

I was sitting on our little balcony facing the setting sun when I heard Tia in the apartment. The box with Mom's ashes rested on the chair beside me. Then the sliding door opened slowly behind me and I moved the box so she could sit down, but continued gazing at the trees.

"Jenna?"

It wasn't Tia. Alex sat down in the other chair. I closed my eyes to avoid meeting his, then opened them again and gave a tentative glance in his direction, focusing on his Adam's apple. He was Korean American and had the most beautiful dark eyes, which were now, unfortunately, off limits.

"Hi," I whispered.

"Are you all right?"

"Yeah."

He scooted his chair closer and took my hand and kissed it. I remembered how lucky I felt when he first asked me out. He was like a dream come true. He could talk about anything and he was witty too, which made being with him so much fun. But ever since my vision of Tia and him in bed, well, I guess you could say I'd crossed him off my list.

"I'm here for you," he said softly.

That's when it really hit me – not only the loss of Alex in my life, but of my life itself. This gift, this curse, made me feel like I was looking through steel bars in a prison cell.

"I think this may take me a while," I said. "And you don't have to wait for me."

I gently withdrew my hand from his, focusing on two large pines swaying in the distance. They reminded me of a couple walking along the seashore at sunset. Which is something I'd hoped Alex and I could do this summer. I had it all planned out – Jekyll Island, a long, romantic weekend, evening walks on the beach, hand in hand, the surf tickling our toes. But my dream had disintegrated.

We sat quietly for a few minutes.

Picking up trash along the Chattahoochee River – that's where we met. I'd signed up for Sweep the Hooch with a couple of friends, thinking it would be cool to help clean up the river bank. It was a brilliant day in early April. I was dressed in jeans, rain boots and a hoodie, using a pick stick to stuff garbage in a plastic bag, when I came upon Alex taking pictures of the river, his bag and stick lying on the ground beside him. He was wearing jeans too, with a long-sleeved blue tee shirt and nice running shoes that were in the process of being ruined by the mud. He paused when he heard me.

"Can't resist," he said, waving his phone.

I smiled and continued searching for trash. He caught up with me and walked beside me, extracting a plastic bag from beneath a bush.

"Is this your first time?" he asked.

"First time on the Chattahoochee but I did it on the Oconee while I was in college. You?"

"Well, I did a story about it last year and thought this time I'd like to actually help out."

"Oh?"

"I'm a TV reporter."

"I'm a teacher and an actress."

"Alex Park," he said, like I should recognize the name.

"Jenna Stevens," I replied, using the same officious tone.

He laughed and I laughed.

I wasn't going to admit he looked familiar and that he was too good looking to be picking up trash, even it was along the scenic Chattahoochee.

We kind of hit it off, talking about the cleanup, the river, our favorite lunch spots – small talk – until he decided to chase another plastic bag just as the breeze lifted it over the water's edge. He reached out to grab it and lost his balance when a rock beneath his foot came loose. He fell into the frigid water, landing on his butt. I couldn't help it. I busted out laughing.

It made me smile to myself remembering how his teeth chattered as he hightailed it back to his car. I thought I'd never see him again since we hadn't exchanged phone numbers or anything. Plus, his phone took a dunking. But he tracked me down, checking with the local school systems until he found a Jenna Stevens.

"Jenna," he said, bringing me back to the present.

But I cut him off with shake of my head and a shrug.

Then he cleared his throat and stood up. He waited for a moment, as though giving me time to change my mind, before leaving me there on the deck by myself, trying not to cry.

5.

"You can't just move out! How am I supposed to pay the rent?"

Tia was standing in the doorway of my room, hands on her hips, still dressed in her school duds – white slacks and a printed pink top.

"Our lease is up in August. I'll pay my rent till then. That'll give you time to find another roommate."

I didn't have to see her face to feel her glaring at me as I packed boxes and bags with clothes, shoes and purses.

"Jenna, what is wrong with you? I know you're grieving but, like, I don't get it. You and your mom weren't even close. And you and me – well, we've been, like, best friends for how long? I can't even remember, it's been so long! You can't just run off and leave me!"

"You've got Alex."

"Alex? Alex is *your* boyfriend, not mine!"

I shook my head, wishing I'd kept my big mouth shut. I

grabbed as much as I could carry and headed for the door. But she didn't step aside.

"Excuse me," I said.

She didn't budge, but I refused to look her in the eye.

"I'm gonna live at my mom's house," I said. "It's mine now."

"Yeah, and you'll be so lonesome."

"No offense, Tia. Now, will you please…"

"You'll get even more depressed than you are now. I know you! And looking at her stuff all the time and living in that God-awful blue house will make you absolutely crazy."

"I'm coming through, one way or another."

Finally, she stepped aside. I lugged two boxes and a bag through the apartment and out to my car, huffing and puffing all the way, then returned for another load.

"And, oh by the way – Alex is just a friend," she said. "All we've talked about is you!"

I hustled to my room, picked up two more boxes and a suitcase and headed out the door again. Then I came back for one final load.

"Jenna! Look at me!"

But I kept moving, picking up a garbage bag filled with stuff and my jewelry box.

"I'm sorry about your mom," she said, almost yelling now. "And I know different people grieve in different ways, but you'll be better off here with me. You know," she said, softening her tone, "friends help friends. You helped me through a rough spot. I want to be there for you too.

Why the hell are you pushing me away?"

The rough spot she was referring to came back to me. It was during ninth grade. I was spending the night at her house. Her dad was watching TV when her mother came home after attending some kind of meeting. At least that's what Tia had told me. But it was after midnight. We were lying in bed whispering about whatever girls whisper about on a sleepover. And then we heard her parents in the living room, her mother yelling: "I am *not* drunk!" Her dad: "It's a miracle you didn't wreck the car." Her mom: "The car is just fine and so am I!" And then there was a crash like a lamp hitting the floor and although it was dark in the bedroom I could hear Tia crying. I put my hand on her shoulder to comfort her. That's when she told me her mom had been fired from her job because she couldn't get out of bed in the morning and was always late for work. And she said she was afraid her parents would divorce. Which they did about a year later.

It was true – we'd been devoted friends. I loved Tia. We'd both had mother problems. But I couldn't stay.

"I just need some space," I said. I knew if I tried to tell her the truth, she'd think I'd gone over the edge, for sure. And if I told her why I was leaving, then I'd have to tell her what I'd seen of her future. I could only imagine how she'd react to that.

"Space? Well, you'll have plenty of space in that over-sized art gallery! Jenna, please don't go."

"The movers will pick up my furniture next week and get it out of your way." I wanted to give her a hug but I knew I'd cry. So I hurried out the door, tossed my stuff in the trunk, hopped in the car and drove away before I could change my mind.

It was true – I didn't want to live in my mother's house with all that blue and green staring me in the face. But I couldn't stand the thought of staying in the apartment with Tia, who I loved more than she knew. How could I watch her descend into that toxic pit? And how could I watch as she and Alex became a whole lot more than "just friends?"

When I arrived at the house, I found my dad sitting on the front step, looking more like a bag of leaves than a human being, his head down, shoulders slumped. God. It was too much.

"Hey, honey," he called, standing and stretching as I climbed out of my car. I automatically checked my reflection in the car window – messy hair, no makeup, sloppy clothes. He was, no doubt, drawing his own conclusions. But the car looked good, I thought. The light blue paint was still like new. Dad had made a big down payment on it for my graduation present, which suddenly came back to me now as I tried to figure out how to avoid talking with him.

A slight breeze wafted the drooping branches of the weeping willow and it dawned on me that Mom planted it as an expression of grief. Her grief over the loss of her marriage and the loss of a normal life. Now the tree was so big, it took up nearly half the front yard.

"Hi, Dad."

I silently reminded myself to look at his ear, his hair, his shoulder. Anything but his eyes.

He hurried over, taking a box from me and followed me inside.

"Upstairs?" he asked.

"Here's fine."

So we set everything in the foyer and he immediately pulled me into a hug – a warm, fatherly hug that felt so good, I could've stayed that way a long time. He kissed the side of my head and rubbed my back a little. And for a fleeting moment, the little girl part of me almost let loose with everything that had happened. I wanted so bad to tell him but he would think I was sick in the head. So I let him believe what I let everyone else believe – that it was grief over Mom's sudden death that was causing my pain.

And finally, he pulled away, gripping my shoulders, examining my face. I focused on his chin.

"Are you all right?"

"Fine, Dad, really. Just, you know, going through the process."

"Tia says you're moving in here?"

"It's a good house," I said, gesturing around the living room. "And fully furnished."

"But, Jenna..."

"Dad, I've made up my mind."

He was staring at me – I could feel it. And I could also tell he was mulling everything over – how much to say, how much not to say, whether he should let me find out the hard way how miserable I'd be. I knew him well enough to know what he was thinking.

"Let's bring in the rest of your stuff," he finally said.

In no time, my boxes and bags were piled in the living room. It was the first time I'd ever seen it look messy. Mom would be appalled.

Not wanting to be rude, but really wishing he'd leave, I stretched out on the couch, making it obvious I was worn out. And that was no lie. He sat down next to me and rubbed my hair and kissed my forehead.

"Come have dinner with me and Meg this weekend."

"Actually, I could use a little help with a very private memorial service."

"How about we sprinkle her ashes in Sweetwater Creek?"

"A creek?"

"Yeah, years ago, she used to love hiking at Sweetwater Creek State Park."

After giving it some thought, I agreed. So, on Saturday we took a short hike along the banks of the stream – just the two of us. We stopped at a scenic spot where the blue water tumbled over large rocks, forming a little waterfall, and I slowly sprinkled Mom's ashes into the creek, watching as the current swept her downstream. We stood there for a while, listening to the birds chattering and the tranquil sound of the water flowing past us.

"She loved you very much," Dad said.

*

Monday morning I returned to school, dropping by for my coffee, as usual, on the way. No premonition this morning. In fact, I felt kind of numb. But I'd been practicing avoiding people's eyes – looking at their hair or their chin – and was pretty confident I was ready.

Maria gave me a hug when I walked in, telling me how sorry she was. And then the students began arriving. First one, then three, then a bunch who got off the first bus. Lots of "Hi, Miss Stevens." And I smiled and greeted them, carefully avoiding looking at their faces. They didn't appear to notice and things were going well until Daisy arrived on the last bus. She ran to me and wrapped her arms around my waist.

"Miss Stevens!" was all she said, but her body language said so much more. I knew she'd missed me, that she felt very close to me. I hugged her back and asked how her mother was doing. I knew her mom had problems and found it hard to hold a job, which made money tight for the family.

"Mama's not feelin' too good," she said, stepping back from me. "But she's not dead like your mama."

The tone of her voice was full of sympathy, so tenderhearted. And I automatically looked down into her sad hazel eyes and was immediately engulfed in that overwhelming sensation that filled my consciousness with one vision after another that I didn't want to see. I saw her being slapped by her mother who looked haggard and old for her years, like maybe she was on drugs or something; then, there was a scene of an overweight teenage Daisy skipping school and hanging out in a house crowded with people. And then she was having a baby. And then another. And another. Then there was a scene of her bailing someone out of jail. And she was old and beaten down before her time, a sick, middle-aged woman staring at a TV screen for hours on end. And I was crying with my hands over my face.

"Miss Stevens? Miss Stevens?"

Her voice sounded like she was standing above me while I was submerged in a swimming pool. Then Maria touched my arm and I realized I was leaning against the wall with my eyes closed. I lunged for my desk, grabbed my purse from the drawer and stumbled from the room into the empty hallway.

"Jenna!" Maria called after me, but I fled like a roach dodging a giant shoe.

No more teaching. No more looking into a sweet child's eyes and seeing a wasted life. No way! With Mom's house and the money she left me I could get by for a while until I figured out what to do next.

When I got home, I headed straight for the bottom kitchen cabinet. Since my mother wasn't one to entertain, I could only assume she was the one who drank the bourbon and the wine. There were two bottles of each and a bottle of whiskey sour mix. Although it wasn't even nine in the morning, I fixed myself a stiff drink and sat down at the kitchen table, trying to calm my nerves.

On the wall in front of me were pictures of Mom's garden in a collage frame, each one focusing on different ripe vegetables. One with bright red tomatoes; another with tall, lush corn stalks; a photo of a plant loaded with green peppers; and another one of green beans.

Then I gazed out the window overlooking her precious garden. Rows of plants were sprouting. I recognized several tomato plants about a foot tall soaking up the sunshine, no tomatoes yet. I was clueless about the small plants in the other rows. My mother had given me an illustrated book on gardening for graduation, which seemed so bizarre at the time. Now I understood. Plants don't have eyes. No windows to their soul. I finished my drink and fixed a second, and then a third before lying down on the sofa and falling into a drunken, dream-filled sleep, where babies and tomatoes mixed together like an abstract painting I didn't understand and didn't like.

6.

A bell was ringing, ringing. I put my hands to my temples, trying to keep my head from exploding. But the ding-donging continued to reverberate through the house and through my brain. I finally opened my eyes and realized I was lying on the sofa. The unbearable noise was the doorbell.

Sunshine streamed through the windows. Meaning it must be mid-afternoon. The doorbell was like the squall of an inconsolable toddler at the table next to yours in a restaurant. While I wanted very much to make the bell stop ringing, the idea of yelling something like "I'm coming" was more than I could bear. And the thought of rushing to the door and opening it was equally repugnant. I steadied myself and stood up slowly, my head swimming. Oh yes – the whiskey sours.

"Jenna!"

It was Dad.

"Are you all right?" he called out.

No, I was not all right. I was about to throw up and I couldn't decide what to do first. Finally, I dragged myself to the door, turned the deadbolt lock and opened it.

"Back in a minute," I mumbled and hurried as quickly as I could, under the circumstances, to the first floor bathroom.

Once the unpleasantness was over and I'd washed my face and rinsed my mouth, I walked carefully back to the living room and sat slowly on my mother's expensive blue sofa. Dad stopped pacing and watched me as I struggled. I really needed to lie down again but I didn't want him to see me, so I sat there staring into space.

"Jenna?"

I waited.

"What the hell is going on?"

I couldn't think of anything to say.

"Talk to me, dammit!"

He was in front of me in a flash, sitting on the coffee table, leaning into my personal space.

"You've been drinking," he said. "Talk to me, Jenna. I'm here for you."

All I wanted to do was zone out.

"Look at me!" he said, touching my chin as though to force me to look up.

I closed my eyes and pushed his hand away.

"Dad, I'm just not feeling too good right now."

"Look at me!"

I rested my head on the cushion.

"I need to sleep."

"You need a cup of coffee, that's what you need."

I slid down until my head was on the arm rest, hoping he would go away.

He jumped up and strode into the kitchen. I heard him muttering under his breath as he opened one cabinet door after another.

"Maria called me," he yelled in an angry voice. "She told me what happened at school. You quit your job?"

I didn't answer.

"You can't just walk out like that. You owe them an explanation. Maria's concerned about you. Tia is too. And I'm worried sick. It's time to stop pushing everyone away and let us help!"

And then he was back in the living room.

"You've got bourbon but you don't have coffee?"

My head felt like it was spinning so I kept my eyes closed. I felt bad not being able to talk with him. But what was I supposed to say?

"God, it's déjà vu all over again," he said. "This is exactly how your mother acted after *her* mother died. You cannot go down the same path. You just can't! I've got a friend who's a psychologist. I'll..."

I sighed.

"This is serious, Jenna! Your mom spiraled into a deep depression after her mother died. And she always seemed to be looking down after that. The woman I'd fallen in love with just kind of disappeared."

I was getting very drowsy.

"I'm not going to let that happen to you," he said.

There was a pause and I could feel him staring at me but I knew better than to open my eyes.

"I'm leaving now. I'll call you tomorrow. So turn on your goddam phone."

He leaned down and kissed my forehead.

"Get up and lock the door! Come on," he said, pulling me by the hands and forcing me to follow him to the door. I dutifully turned the deadbolt and sank back onto the couch, relieved to be alone again.

*

Rehearsals began the next evening and I was almost ready to leave when the doorbell chimed. I was hoping it wasn't Dad again. Turned out it was someone else I didn't want to face. Through the peephole I could see Alex holding a bouquet of flowers. I considered not answering but decided to open the door, looking immediately at the pink lilies.

"Alex."

"Hope you've got a vase."

"I'm sure I do somewhere. Come in."

I took the flowers and headed to the kitchen, motioning for him to follow.

"I was on my way out the door," I said. "Rehearsals start tonight for the play I'm in. But I've got a minute."

I rummaged through a couple of cabinets near the back door till I found what I was looking for. It was good to have something to do so I didn't have to look at him. I removed the plastic wrapper from the flowers and slipped them into the vase, filling it halfway with water from the tap.

"Congratulations on getting such a big part," he said.

"Thanks. I have to admit I'm a little nervous."

I arranged the flowers a bit and then set them on the kitchen table.

"You doing okay?" he asked.

"Yeah, I think so. The flowers are gorgeous."

"I can't wait to see the play."

"I'm excited," I said, looking in his general direction and trying for a smile.

"I know you have to go but I sure would like to see you sometime. Maybe dinner or lunch or something."

I didn't need to look into his very fine eyes to know his face was filled with sympathy and affection. Before I could think how to answer, he closed the distance between us and wrapped his arms around me. It was not a passionate embrace, but a warm hug. He didn't try to kiss me. He just held me close.

"I'm so sorry, Jenna."

We stood like that for a moment and it took all my willpower not to hug him back. In spite of the vision I'd had of him and Tia, I knew he was a good guy. The kind of guy who had made me consider a long-term relationship, maybe even marriage. But he deserved a lot better than what I had to offer.

"I really appreciate your coming." And I pulled away. "I've gotta get going. Don't wanna be late."

I led the way back through the living room to the front

door, which was still standing open.

"I'll keep in touch," I said.

My eyes were focused on his bobbing Adam's apple.

"Oh, I almost forgot," he said. "I brought you something else."

And he extracted a small, framed picture from his jacket and handed it to me. It was a photo of the two of us that Tia had taken with her phone as we were heading out the door on our second date. His arm was around me and we both looked unbelievably happy and carefree. Tia told me later that we made a cute couple. And she was right. Of course, he was so good-looking, he would make any couple look cute – didn't matter who he had his arm around.

"I still feel the same way," he whispered.

He walked down the front steps and I eased the door closed behind him.

*

Immersing myself in the play was a relief. I spent hours practicing my lines and was off book before anyone else. Everyone was professional and seemed to get along. It was tiring, but in a good way. I could only imagine how fatigued some of the others must've been who had day jobs.

As we were gathering our things after the first week of rehearsals Sam invited me to join him and some others for drinks. I thought most of us were going but it turned out it was just Sam, me, my stage husband, Randall, and Melanie, who played the part of my sister Lily in the play. We walked to an upscale bar called The Jazz Tavern and found a table. It was crowded on a Saturday night with a jazz trio in the corner, making for a nice vibe. We ordered snacks and drinks and Randall and Melanie gabbed a lot about the play.

"It's so meaningful," she gushed in her high voice, dipping flatbread into hummus dip. "I mean, it's all about life, you know?"

Melanie was a little older than me and a little shorter than me. Pretty shoulder-length dark brown hair, brown eyes and a way of sounding sincere even when she was talking about something as mundane as shopping for groceries.

She took a bite and nodded at Randall, who sipped his beer and turned his attention to Sam.

"So how'd you get this directing gig? I mean, you're the youngest director I've ever worked with."

"Connections. Of course, I've been directing since I was in high school. A lot of experience. But my uncle's on the Midtown Theatre board. The director they originally hired backed out. So my uncle recommended me. And voila!"

Randall nodded and took another drink. He knew all about connections. I had the feeling that's the only reason he'd come to the bar. He was on a fact-finding mission. And I wasn't at all surprised when he announced a moment later he had to get going.

"Yeah, me too," Melanie piped up, wiping her mouth with a napkin as she cocked her head at Randall. "Would you mind walking me to my car?"

She pulled a compact and a tube of lipstick from her purse and proceeded to paint her lips deep pink as Randall tossed a twenty on the table.

"I don't have any cash," Melanie confessed, shrugging innocently at Sam and me. There was something about her that reminded me of a college girl begging her mother to pay for concert tickets because she'd already spent her own money on a trip to the beach. "Can I pay you back tomorrow?"

And they were gone, Melanie clutching Randall's arm as they threaded their way through the crush of people.

Sam downed the last of his sangria and glanced around, searching for our waitress. He looked younger tonight. I don't know why. And I wondered how I looked to him. I was wearing a teal shirt, sleeves rolled up to my elbows and skinny khakis. My hair was down on my shoulders. Lip gloss, minimal makeup.

"Want another?" he asked.

"Sure."

I was having whiskey sours, mostly because I didn't want a beer and didn't know what else to order. And he motioned for the waitress to bring each of us a second drink. When he did, I noticed a tattoo peeking from beneath the right sleeve of his tee shirt. I couldn't see the design but I latched onto that image, deciding I didn't like it.

"I've noticed you're using Rachel's mannerisms," he said.

I'd watched Rachel closely when she was onstage as the older version of Rose. And there were certain hand movements she made and a way of tilting her head slightly that I'd adopted. It was nice that Sam noticed.

I smiled and nodded.

"Do you two ever talk?" he asked.

"Sometimes. But she's busy practicing her lines."

"Yeah, she works hard. So do you."

"Well, I try."

I ate one of the little flatbreads, mostly for something to do. And then the waitress brought our drinks. She set the sangria in front of me and the whiskey sour in front of him.

"So what do you do for fun?" he said, switching the drinks.

I smiled self-consciously, not really knowing how to answer.

"You do occasionally have some fun, right?" he continued. "Bowling? Skating? Dancing? Hiking, maybe? Bicycling? Am I getting warm?"

He was flirting with me. And I really didn't want to go there. It could spoil everything. And, besides, he had that tattoo and drank sangria.

"I'm kind of stodgy, actually," I said. "I read a lot and do a little gardening."

One exaggeration and one lie.

"You are *so* not stodgy."

He sipped his drink and studied me, probably deciding whether I was worth further attention.

"I like to read too," he said, a twinkle in his eye. "Especially if it's a scintillating book. But I also like camping and hiking and that kind of stuff. I'm thinking about an outing to Amicalola Falls."

This is where I was supposed to say something like: "Wow, I'd love to see the falls." But I just nodded. Under different circumstances I might've been interested in getting to know him better. We obviously had a love of theater in common. And I had to admit, the thought of going hiking in a scenic spot with someone interesting held great appeal. But I still felt this attachment to Alex, even though I knew he was already moving on.

I bit my tongue and turned to listen as the musicians launched into *Take Five*, one of my favorite jazz tunes.

7.

Dad had all but ordered me to come for dinner and I decided it would be a good opportunity to reassure him I was all right so he would back off. As I pulled into the driveway I was fairly confident I could handle being with him and Meg. I was getting pretty good at avoiding direct eye contact without being obvious.

Their house was what my mother once described in "real estate speak" as a cozy cottage on the edge of the historic Druid Hills neighborhood. Walking distance to the CDC for Dad and to Emory Hospital, where Meg was a research nurse. Her hobby was working in the yard and it showed. A pretty stone path lead to the front porch, bordered by clumps of pink calla lilies, purple tulips and white delphiniums. Garden gnomes peeked around the flowers, making me feel like I was walking through a children's storybook.

Meg answered the door wearing a loose yellow top

over black leggings, reminding me of a plump bumble bee. She hugged me and led the way to the kitchen where she was in the middle of tossing a big bowl of salad. The appetizing aroma tipped me off that her excellent chicken tetrazzini was in the oven. I handed her a bottle of white wine I'd found at Mom's house.

"The corkscrew is in the drawer," she said, pointing.

"Not sure I know how to do this," I replied, trying to figure out whether the handles should be up or down. "It was always cheap wine with screw-off caps in college."

"Tom!" she called out. "Need a man's touch in here!"

Dad appeared, looking his usual good-looking, casual self in khaki shorts and a striped polo. He took the corkscrew from me and had the wine open so fast, I couldn't follow his technique. He poured the two of us a glass but I noticed he didn't pour one for Meg. Why they were keeping the pregnancy a secret was beyond me.

"Anything simple I can do to help?" I asked.

"Set the table?" she suggested.

I took the stack of dishes, napkins and silverware already sitting on the counter and headed for the table while Dad put ice in the water glasses. But when I arranged the plates I realized there were four.

"Someone else coming?"

"Oh, yeah," Dad said. "Our neighbor Janet Willer. I think you met her before. Auburn hair, glasses, very nice."

"Can't remember."

I was surprised they'd invited someone else. But it might make it easier since they wouldn't be completely focused on me.

And then the doorbell buzzed and Dad escorted Janet into the kitchen. She was as Dad described her but taller than I expected. She was dressed in a colorful, long broomstick skirt and peasant top.

"Home-made lemon ice box pie," she announced in a deep, smoker's voice, setting the pie on the counter and turning to me. "Jenna, so good to see you again. I don't know if you remember but we met at the wedding."

She reached out to shake my hand and I played along, looking her in the eye. She had a rather intense gaze, magnified, quite literally by her thick glasses. Her smile made it seem as though she really was glad to be there with us. So I assumed she lived alone.

"You're even prettier than I remembered," she gushed.

"Thank you," Dad said.

"Like you had anything to do with it," Janet cried.

"Well, I did," he said.

And everyone laughed.

The dinner was scrumptious, the conversation was light and I was doing pretty well. It made it easier that I could look at Janet, although it sometimes felt like she was a little too interested in me. She asked what it was like being a teacher and about my role in the play. And then, as we were having our pie in the living room, she told me how sorry she was about my mom.

"I lost my mother when I was young, too," she said. "It was very hard on me."

The way she raised her eyebrows made it seem as

though she was observing me, waiting for me to open up. I could feel Dad and Meg studying me as well. It was like a game of chess and they were waiting to see if I would put my queen in play. And that's when suspicion welled up from my gut to my brain.

I nodded and sipped my wine, then excused myself to visit the bathroom. As soon as I closed the door behind me, I pulled out my phone and did a search for Janet Willer, Atlanta. Sure enough, topping the results – Dr. Janet Willer, clinical psychologist.

My first impulse was to stalk back into the living room and let Dad have it. My hand was on the doorknob. But I forced myself to take a deep breath. What would it accomplish besides making him even more worried. So I flushed the toilet, washed my hands, freshened my lip gloss and forced myself to continue the charade. I played it cool for another thirty minutes, then thanked them profusely as I made my exit.

Dad was, no doubt, getting a full analysis before I even backed out of the driveway.

*

The field trip to Glendale Arms was something Rachel cooked up. She was the elderly version of Rose in the play – the character who had an adjoining room with her sister Lily at a retirement home. It was their memories that Melanie and I acted out as younger versions of the sisters. Rachel decided it would help her performance to visit an assisted living home. I figured it might help me too so I tagged along. Helen, who played the older Lily, said she didn't need to do that much research. And Melanie wasn't interested either.

As we signed in at the front desk I was having second thoughts, myself. A man in an obvious toupee was snoring, his chin on his chest, in one of the lobby chairs. Two women with tight, grey curls stared at us from a loveseat. A woman with a walker slowly approached us and said "can you help me find my house?"

"Mrs. Whitmire," a staff member said in a booming voice, "You ready to play Bingo?"

The old woman shuffled away, pushing her walker ahead of her.

Rachel had arranged for us to visit with a pair of real sisters. Just like the characters in the play, they had adjoining rooms. A lady behind the desk escorted us to a second floor activity area where we found a small group of residents sitting at long tables with green plastic tablecloths, listening to an elderly woman with a purse dangling from her shoulder play the piano. There were two women sitting together by the front windows, one of them singing along. I followed Rachel to their table and our guide introduced us.

"Miss Frances, Miss Betty, you have some visitors. Isn't that nice?"

Her tone was syrupy like she was talking to pre-schoolers.

"This is Frances," she said, gesturing to the woman who'd been singing, dressed in a blue floral jacket. "And this is Betty," she said, waving at the other woman in a tan sweater. And then she rushed off.

"Very nice to meet you," said Rachel as we sat down across from them. "My name is Rachel and this is Jenna."

They smiled at us and Frances resumed singing.

"I remember that song from when I was a little girl," Rachel said. "*Que sera sera.*"

Frances stopped singing and smiled.

"It's one of my favorite songs," she said.

"It's a stupid song," Betty complained, scowling.

"It's not stupid," said Frances, looking hurt.

"Is too," said Betty.

They both had fluffy white hair and glasses, but there was no sisterly resemblance.

"Why do you think it's a stupid song?" Rachel asked.

"What song?" Betty said.

"*Que sera sera,*" said Rachel.

"That's a stupid song," Betty replied, rolling her eyes.

"It is not," said Frances.

"Is too," said Betty.

"Well, why do you think it's stupid?" Rachel persisted.

"Because it's so… because it's… lazy," Betty said.

"You mean fatalistic?" Rachel asked.

The old sisters both looked at her with quizzical expressions.

"*Que sera sera,*" Rachel persevered. "You think it's a fatalistic philosophy of life?"

"Good grief," said Betty. "It means whatever will be, will be and there's nothing you can do about it. What a stupid thing to say."

"It's not stupid," said Frances, looking like she was about to cry.

"Is too," said Betty.

The music ended abruptly and Frances shifted around so she could see the woman sitting at the piano who was now staring into space.

"Why don't you play *Que sera sera?*" she called out. "It's my favorite song and I haven't heard it in years. Do you know how to play it?"

"I'm leaving," said Betty. "I can't stand that song."

And she struggled out of her chair.

"I don't know if I remember..." said the piano lady.

"It goes like this," Frances said cheerfully, launching into the chorus.

The woman at the piano played along with her, not missing a note as Frances sang loudly. Her sister pushed her walker toward the hallway, shaking her head in disgust.

I was intrigued, wondering if Frances and Betty disagreed on a lot of things. So I got contact information for the old sisters' families. Turns out Frances, the one who liked the song, believed everything happened for a reason. Her daughter said when her brother was killed in Viet Nam, her mom said "it was God's will." Which the daughter said made it seem like her brother's life was only important in how it fit into the larger scheme of things.

As for Betty, the one who called the song stupid, her son said she was a nurse at the V.A. Hospital and volunteered as a mentor to low-income teenage girls, trying to keep them in school. He said her nephew's death in Viet Nam made her angry and when she retired she joined Grandmothers for Peace.

Fascinating – the sisters were so different. Frances's philosophy was apparently to do the best you can with a pair of Jacks. Betty's was to return some cards to the dealer and draw some new ones in hopes of getting a royal flush.

Of course, it made me think about my "gift." Mom said there was no way to change what you saw in someone's future. But what if she was wrong? What if Betty was right – you keep trying to get better cards than the ones you're dealt.

8.

Mr. Spencer replied to my email right away, agreeing to meet me for coffee. I hadn't thanked him for the flowers he sent after Mom died, so it was a good excuse to contact him. But that wasn't my real reason for wanting to talk.

He'd done his best to be a good dad to Tia and her brother as his marriage crumbled. He won custody, I'm sure, because of Mrs. Spencer's alcohol problem. So I'd seen him many times over the years and he always welcomed me into their home as though I were one of the family.

He was already there when I arrived at the coffee shop, sitting at a table on the patio. He stood up as I approached. He was a handsome middle-aged man, tall and trim with only the slightest hint of a paunch, dressed in brown slacks and a tweedy sport coat. He looked like the successful businessman he was, with a touch of grey at the temples and the same creamy brown complexion Tia had.

"Jenna, how you doing, honey?"

"Mr. Spencer, so good to see you again."

He gave me a fatherly hug, then dashed inside to place our order while I sat down at the table, which was bathed in late morning sunlight. He was back in a moment with two coffees and a large muffin, which he cut in half to share.

"Tia told me you got a role in a play," he said.

"At the Midtown Theatre. It's called *Rose and Lily*. I get to play Rose as a young woman."

"How exciting," he said, sipping his coffee.

He was carefully avoiding anything negative, waiting for me to get to the point of our meeting.

He asked about my dad and Meg. I asked how Tia's older brother, Terry, was doing. I thanked him for the bouquet he'd sent. Small talk as we ate the muffin and enjoyed our coffee. And finally, I worked up the nerve to share what was on my mind.

"So, I guess you're wondering why I wanted to see you."

He gave a friendly shrug.

"Well, I'm sure Tia told you I moved out of the apartment. I'm living at my mom's house now. Anyway, I feel bad about leaving her alone. I want you to know that. I love her like a sister, maybe more. And I miss her too. It's just that… well, I just need some time on my own to kind of sort things out."

He nodded slowly.

"But that's not why I wanted to talk with you. You see, I'm a little concerned about Tia because of her mother's alcohol problem."

His eyebrows furrowed then.

"I've read that alcoholism can be inherited," I continued. "And I'm hoping that doesn't happen to Tia. But you know, when you're in college everyone's drinking. I mean, everybody's doing it. And I should've thought about it way before now. But I was a stupid college kid and it didn't cross my mind back then that maybe I should discourage her from drinking since she might have a gene for it or something."

Actually, Tia and I didn't drink much in college but we were surrounded by people who did. So the words coming out of my mouth were true, technically speaking. But I was fudging big time on the implication. Hopefully, for a good cause.

"Have you noticed her drinking too much?" he asked.

How should I put it, I thought, without being dishonest?

"Well, I'm not saying she's a lush or anything. But there's always a couple of bottles in the cabinet and going out always includes drinks. And it's just that she's so young. I'm just worried it might get worse as she gets older. And I was wondering if that's kind of how it started with Mrs. Spencer."

Which took him by surprise, I think.

"Well," he said, setting his cup down. He squinted like he was thinking back and shifted in his chair, nodding his head as if to himself. "I suppose that's how it began. You're right – there's a lot of drinking going on in college. Seems normal. And even after college, seems like drinking is just part of going out. And Portia's drinking problem kind of snuck up on me. I finally realized how serious it was when I found a bottle of vodka inside one of her purses on a shelf in her closet. She had about ten purses stored in there and I was looking for my fanny pack so I could wear it to a Falcons game. I thought she might've put it with her pocketbooks, you know. And this old brown handbag was very heavy and I looked inside it to see what in the world was in there and lo, and behold, there was a fifth of Smirnoff. I stood there with that bottle in my hand wondering 'what the hell?' And then it dawned on me that the only reason someone would hide a bottle of liquor is so someone else wouldn't know about it. And then I thought about the way she talked about the price of groceries going up all the time and about how tired she was in the evenings and how hard it was for her to wake up in the morning and about how she was always popping a breath mint in her mouth."

He sat there staring out at the trees in the distance as the cars whizzed by.

"Hm," he said.

Finally, he drew a deep breath and looked at me.

"Jenna, I'm glad you decided to talk with me. I don't know if Tia has a problem or whether she might develop one but it's worth discussing with her. Although I don't think I'll mention your name. I do think it's interesting you're both concerned about each other but can't seem to talk with each other about those concerns."

He raised his eyebrows at me.

I nodded sheepishly and then changed the subject. Tia said her dad had hired a professional genealogist to do a family history who dug up all kinds of fascinating information. So I told him I was interested in doing the same thing – which was true, although for different reasons – and got the name of his genealogist.

I set up an appointment with her, figuring if I could find some family history of early deaths that might possibly be from cancer or heart disease or something, that might be ammunition to get Dad to take better care of himself and get tested.

*

With three more rehearsals before the show opened, the mood was not as relaxed onstage as it had been early on. It wasn't that we didn't know our lines, but Sam was putting pressure on us to really inhabit our roles, to make the characters come alive.

"I want to feel your anger," he shouted. Or "make me cry here, make me cry!" And "you want the audience to laugh out loud on that line – don't throw it away!"

It was during the flashback scene where Rose falls in love with her husband-to-be that the shit hit the fan.

We were standing next to a fence post, backlit by romantic moonlight. His hands were on my waist as I gazed shyly into Randall's eyes.

"You are so beautiful," he said.

"It's gotta be about more than beauty, Pete."

"It is. It is."

"Because beauty fades."

"It's the beauty inside that lasts," he said, leaning down and kissing me softly on the mouth.

That scene had never bothered me up until that moment. But there was something about the way he kissed me – it felt so real. I guess he was taking Sam's direction to heart. And it reminded me of the way Alex kissed me. And while I was normally very focused on my scenes and my lines, I think I was totally absorbed in Rose's character at that moment – her yearning for true love. Of course, I was longing to turn back the clock, longing to kiss Alex again. And that's when a tingling began in my gut as Randall gazed intently into my eyes.

"I love you, Rose. And I want you to marry me."

The overwhelming feeling of the visionsight swamped my senses. Scenes flashed through my mind, fast-forwarding from one to the next. Randall and Melanie having sex in the dressing room. Then there was sex with another young actress in another play, and another and another. And after each one, he returned home to his wife and gave her a peck on the cheek, telling her how long rehearsal had lasted and how tired he was. When I came to, I was holding tightly to the fence post and Randall was staring down at me like I was crazy.

"What the hell's going on?" Sam yelled from the darkened theater.

"She's having a fit or something," said Randall.

"No," I said. "I'm fine. Just a little dizzy for a moment."

My voice sounded weak and quivery so I tried again.

"I'm okay."

I peered into the darkness and nodded my head vigorously.

"All right. Do it!" Sam replied.

So I took a deep breath and we picked up right after the kiss.

"I love you, Rose. And I want you to marry me."

Still feeling weak and shaky, I was careful not to look directly into Randall's eyes. I gazed as lovingly as I could at his eyebrows.

"Well, I have to admit you're a good-looking man, you've got a good job and you're a pretty good dancer," I said, trying to sound like I was teasing him.

"What more could you want?" he said.

But before I could say my next line he dropped out of character.

"You have to look in my eyes, Jenna. I can't get into it if you're looking at the ceiling or whatever the fuck you're doing."

"Let's take five," Sam shouted. "Randall, why don't you get a Coke or something."

He headed toward the back as Sam sprinted up the steps to join me center stage.

"What's going on?"

He sounded concerned, not angry. But there was an element of stress there too, like it was a bad time for anything to come up at this point in rehearsals.

"I'm fine, really."

"Well, you have to look him in the eye."

"Right."

"You're not looking at me either," he said, pushing his horn-rimmed glasses to the top of his head.

"Sorry. I think I just need to eat a cereal bar or something. My blood sugar level must be low."

"Jenna!" he barked.

I met his gaze then. He was staring hard into my eyes as though he was searching for something.

"You're a damn good actress. You've got a strong stage presence. You make me feel your emotions. And you've got the looks to get lead roles. Nothing but good things coming down the pike. So don't get nervous. And don't let Randall bother you."

He thought I was having a case of nerves.

"Thanks," I whispered, and took a deep breath.

"But Randall's right. Comprende?"

"Si."

I got a Snickers bar from the snack machine before we continued. I needed some quick energy. It was troubling that I'd had a vision with someone I cared nothing about. It's true, I'd been focused on getting into character. And although a feeling of regret had certainly welled up about Alex, still, it wasn't supposed to happen like this. At least not according to my mother. It had to be that I was trying so hard to really feel the moment, like Sam wanted. I decided before we came back on Monday I would figure out how to gaze lovingly into Randall's eyes while, deep down inside, hating his guts. It also bothered me that I recognized his wife in my vision. She was the nervous actress I'd seen in the lobby on my callback, the one who didn't get the part.

The rest of the rehearsal went off without a problem. As I was heading out the door afterwards, Sam called for me to wait up.

"Tomorrow is Sunday," he said. "No rehearsal. I wanna go to Amicalola Falls. Need someone to go with. So I'll be at your place at nine. We'll get a biscuit and coffee on the way out of town. It'll be a great way to relax before tech rehearsal Tuesday night."

Before I could beg off, he spoke again.

"Wear hiking boots or good walking shoes. I've got sunscreen and bug repellent. I'm fixing peanut butter and jelly sandwiches. If you've got any food you think might work, bring it. See you at nine."

"But…"

He waved at me and trotted up the aisle between sections A and B.

"Sam!" I called out, but he ignored me and disappeared through the door to the lobby.

9.

I clicked on Sam's number five or six times that night. But I never hit "send." Instead, I hauled my messy pile of stuff from the foyer to the guest room upstairs. I'd been pulling things from the stack ever since I moved in, kind of like a dumpster diver, grabbing a pair of shoes or rummaging through suitcases for a pair of pants. Couldn't bring myself to unpack and settle in. That would make it seem permanent. So now the pile was still an ugly jumble, but at least it was out of sight.

As I lay on the sofa with a throw over me, I checked my messages. One from Alex, one from Tia and two from Dad. Alex left a voicemail saying he couldn't wait to see the show. His voice was so sincere and so velvety. I always liked his voice. Deep, but not too deep, manly but not overly macho, intelligent but not geeky. Then he said he might bring Tia to the play. Wonderful.

The text from Tia was particularly annoying: "My

father said you guys had coffee. What the hell? And, oh, by the way, you're a real twit for dumping Alex. He's, like, the perfect man. So, muchas gracias for making him available." I heaved an angry sigh as I clicked on my dad's first text: "how r u?" And the second one said: "Call me." So I texted him about my outing with Sam to ease his mind, then turned off my phone, furious with Tia and Alex.

The next morning, I made sure I was ready early. I studied my reflection in the mirror. Khaki shorts, pale green tee, running shoes, white visor. My hair was pulled back in a ponytail to keep it off my neck, knowing I'd get hot and sweaty. No makeup, other than pink lip gloss and sunscreen. My sling bag was packed with two bottles of water, cereal bars, two apples, a bag of baby carrots and two little packs of trail mix, all of which I picked up on my way home from rehearsal.

A quick check of the living room. Too tidy, I decided. So I dropped a couple of magazines on the floor, got a glass from the kitchen and set it on the coffee table and turned one of the cushions a little sideways. And that's when the doorbell rang.

"Fancy," Sam said when I opened the door. "Ready?"

I grabbed my backpack and locked the door.

"Where's your car?" I asked, looking toward the street.

"Don't have one. A friend dropped me off."

"Well, then, I guess we'll take mine."

We got biscuits and coffee in the McDonald's drive-through, although I would've preferred bagels and coffee from Panera. And we talked pretty much non-stop all the way – about an hour and a half drive – about the plays he'd directed, the plays he wanted to direct, about some of the actors he'd worked with, what he liked in an actor, how he was building his resume, that kind of thing. Then I could feel him giving me the once over.

"You're fun to talk with," he said.

I couldn't help it – I laughed out loud.

"What?" he said.

I just smiled and kept my eyes on the road.

"Oh," he said, chuckling. "Well, it's true. You're a good listener."

*

We walked past a reflecting pool and along the stream to the base of the falls. The highest east of the Mississippi, the sign said. And there it was, stunning to look at, water shimmering in the sunshine as it cascaded onto the jutting rocks. Amicalola was a Cherokee word that meant "tumbling waters." And it was a perfect description. It was actually a series of falls more than 700 feet high. We followed some other people up a winding wooden staircase – 175 steps – to a deck with a glorious view.

There were so many trees all around – oak, birch, hickory, poplar – that I wondered what it would look like in the fall.

I snapped some pictures on my phone but who would I share them with? There was a time when I would've posted them online for friends to see, but not anymore. So I put my phone away and just soaked up the beauty.

It was another 400 steps to the top, so we decided to

head back down to the car so we could drive up. Once we were at the precipice, we gazed out over the crest of the falls, the mountains in the distance.

"Gorgeous," he said.

"Yeah," I agreed. But I was imagining myself falling into the water and plunging over the edge to the outcrop below. In fact, that's not unlike what I was doing in my life – bobbing along in a stream that becomes a river that rushes toward a precipice. The water has no choice but to cascade over the brink. And, right now, it was as though I was trapped in a current, being pulled along with the rushing water, straight for a waterfall.

I shook my head, trying to banish the morbid thought. I wanted to seize the day. I studied Sam's face, which seemed to embody everything I aspired to – self-assurance and an enthusiastic outlook on life.

My sunglasses kept him from seeing exactly where I was looking, which at that moment was his lips. Part of me wanted to kiss those lips – I'd been feeling so isolated. But I was keeping my shades on, just in case. The episode the night before with Randall had spooked me. I wasn't sure anymore how much or how little affection I had to feel for someone to have a visionsight. And, truth be told, I was hurt that Alex was abandoning me much more quickly than I would've guessed.

That's when Sam took my hand.

"Let's go for a little hike," he said, pulling me with him.

We headed down a path into the forest, enjoying the spectacular vistas as they opened up. It felt good to be outside. My skin craved sunshine. I dawdled when we came to each clearing, lifting my face to the sun.

After finding a log to sit on, we opened our packs. Sam kept his promise, making peanut butter and jelly sandwiches. With the apples and baby carrots I'd brought, it was a decent picnic.

"You excited about opening night?" he asked between bites.

"And a little nervous."

"No need to be. You'll do great. And I think audiences are gonna really like it, really respond. If we don't need to make any tweaks, I'll be heading for Charlotte after the first two shows."

"You're leaving?"

"Yeah, I've been hired as Artistic Director at the Lyric Theatre there."

Surprise must've been written all over my face.

"You knew I was leaving, right?" he said.

"Well…"

"My first play will be *Funerals*. Written by a local play-wright. Very edgy. Then, my second play will be more conventional. We're doing *Steel Magnolias*. And I want you to be in it. You'd be a good Annelle."

"Me?"

"Yeah, when the run is over here, you can join me. I'm thinking we might make compatible roommates."

I took another bite of my apple and stared up through the lush green leaves as they whispered in the breeze, probably talking about us.

"I found an apartment close to the theater," he continued. "Two bedrooms. One for me, one for you. Though I was thinking a little hanky-panky might be pleasant."

He smiled one of his mischievous smiles. I was still wearing my shades but they couldn't hide the blush spreading over my cheeks.

"I like you a lot, Jenna. And I'm thinking maybe you like me too."

I was trying not to choke as I swallowed that bite of apple. He quickly gathered our stuff and pulled me deeper into the woods until we could no longer see the path. Then he leaned against a tree, dropped the backpacks and drew me close. His hands were on my waist and then his lips were on mine. It was a tantalizing kiss and I found myself returning it. He kissed my neck and caressed me. My hands were roaming over his body too. I was amazed I was going along with him and knew that in another moment we'd both have our pants down right there in the woods. I forced myself to push away.

Sam just smiled that same naughty smile as before.

"Yeah, you like me," he said. "Come on."

He took my hand and drew me further into the forest. We had sex on the ground in a small clearing. When he reached up and pulled my sunglasses off, I couldn't resist gazing into his bewitching blue eyes. I was relieved and stunned I didn't see his future.

10.

Don't ask me why, but meeting with the genealogist made me feel like a spy. Her name was Ethel Robertson. She was a plump black woman with a short salt and pepper Afro and big hoop earrings, fashionably dressed, with a friendly, expressive face. We met in her home, a charming old house in the gentrified Candler Park neighborhood.

To break the ice, I asked how she got into genealogy.

"Well, at first, I just wanted to find out about my own family history," she explained. "But it was so fascinating, I just kept doing more and more research. You wouldn't believe how much I found out about my ancestors. I won't bore you with all the details, but suffice it to say I was shocked at how much European blood I've got." She laughed heartily. "Then I started doing family histories for friends and they said, 'Ethel, you oughta hang out your shingle.' And I thought – why not? So I took some classes and got my certificate and now it's my business. And I just love what I do."

Which made me smile.

"Of course, at first I just did research for black families," she went on. "But I've expanded way beyond that now. I do genealogies for all colors!" And she laughed again.

She wasn't the studious researcher I'd expected. I liked her right away.

"So, do you know very much about your ancestors, where they came from?" she asked.

"I'm ashamed to admit I've never taken much of an interest until now."

"Well, don't feel bad. Most people don't get around to it until they're in their fifties. So you're ahead of the curve. Now, did you bring some names and dates with you?"

I fumbled in my bag for an index card I'd brought along.

"Think I'll need more than that," she said, chuckling.

She typed my email address into her phone and said she'd send me a fill-in-the-blank list. I gave her a retainer check and left, with high hopes she'd find something I could use to help save my dad's life.

*

Opening night was sold out and I had a serious case of nerves. Of course, I was excited too. Sam popped his head into the women's dressing room and made some encourag-ing remarks but I can't remember what he said. Melanie was talking a mile a minute to no one in particular. Rachel and Helen were very professional, chatting quietly as they sat for makeup.

As for me, I kept running my lines over and over,

reminding myself to focus. I knew I couldn't risk looking into Randall's eyes, regardless of what Sam told me. I would look at his eyebrow, his cheek bone, his nostril, but not his eyes. If I had a visionsight episode in front of a sold-out house, my career as an actress would be over.

Thankfully, the play opened with the older sisters on stage, arguing about who said what, when they were younger. Rachel and Helen were totally in character, delivering their lines perfectly.

"You remember the night David proposed to me?" Helen asked, just the right little giggle in her voice as the sister named Lily.

"How could I forget?" Rachel replied, with the perfect amount of sarcasm for Rose.

And the lights faded on the two of them as Melanie and I strolled center stage. Thankfully, the adrenaline kicked in.

"Isn't he the handsomest man you've ever seen?" Melanie gushed, closing her eyes dreamily.

"You're not gonna marry that guy, are you?" I said, cocking my head sideways in disbelief.

"And what's wrong with David?" she shot back. "He's better looking than Pete."

"I know it's your philosophy of life, Lily, and I really hate to break it to you but looks are not everything!"

"I know you, Rose. You're just jealous. You wish you had a man as sweet and good-looking as..."

"All I'm saying," I interrupted, "is that we'll see who's happier ten years from now. At least Pete has a career ahead of him."

"Well, you can marry for money if you want to. I'm marrying for love!"

And Melanie flounced off stage, leaving me rolling my eyes.

God, the electricity that flowed from that audience! They laughed at just the right times, and even some moments we didn't expect, and they cried at the right times too. And when the show was over we got a standing ovation that gave me a buzz, the likes of which I'd never experienced. I felt like an uncorked bottle of expensive champagne.

I was in my underwear when Sam burst into the dressing room, hugging everyone and kissing them on the cheek, including me. He seemed oblivious to my state of undress. Melanie giggled as she slipped on her jeans and Rachel and Helen were exuberant as well.

When I emerged from backstage, I was still on cloud nine as I made my way to the auditorium. So I was taken by surprise when I found Alex waiting for me with a big bouquet, smiling warmly as I approached. I thought he would hand me the flowers, but instead, he set them on the edge of the stage and wrapped his arms around me. For a split second, I wanted to hug him too. He smelled so good and felt so good, with his chest against mine. I almost forgot our romance was over. Then he backed away and I came to my senses.

"You were wonderful, Jenna! Amazing. I couldn't believe it was really you – you were so convincing. I thought you were gonna slap your husband's face in that one scene. You looked so angry."

"I'm so glad you liked it."

"Liked it? I loved it! I was awestruck. Great play. Super performances. Especially yours."

He was looking directly at me and there was a part of me that wanted to look into his eyes. But the thought of seeing his future with Tia – and who knows what other horrible things – was too much to bear.

"Where's Tia?" I said.

"She had a photo shoot, but I couldn't wait. I've missed you."

"The flowers are lovely," I said, picking them up. "I don't suppose you've seen my dad." And I made a show of looking around the auditorium. "No, I guess you haven't met him, have you?"

"Jenna," he said, touching my arm.

I put my nose in the flowers to breathe in their scent, avoiding his gaze. It was hard being this close to him.

"Maybe after you talk with your Dad, we could go for a drink or maybe a smoothie?"

"Actually, the cast is going to a pub together."

"How about lunch tomorrow?"

"Lunch?"

"We could meet at Panera?"

"Believe it or not, I've got an appointment with a genealogist tomorrow for lunch. I'm hiring her to do a family history." It wasn't totally lying, was it? I mean I did meet with a genealogist. The meeting could just as well have been tomorrow.

He took a breath as though he was about to say something. But then he swallowed and it was gone.

"Dad and Meg are around here somewhere," I said and headed up the stairs.

When we got to the lobby, they were waiting for me with another bouquet of flowers, although not as elaborate as the one Alex had given me. I introduced them and Alex quickly said his farewells.

"Enjoy your cast party," he said as he walked away, a definite note of sarcasm in his voice.

"He's even better looking in person than he is on the news," Meg said as he hurried out the front door.

"Yeah," said Dad. "Well, you know what I mean."

"Stop it," I said.

They both laughed conspiratorially.

"Jenna, I just want you to know," Dad said, "that you were awesome, fantastic, mesmerizing!"

And he hugged me close, which, I have to admit, felt really good.

"Everything your dad said, and then some," Meg said. And she hugged me too.

"Thanks."

"I just didn't realize what an actress you are," Dad went on. "I have to admit I thought this was just a hobby for you. But now I get it. Congratulations!"

It warmed my heart to hear him say it.

"The scene when you and your husband are having it out about the kids – wow! That was really powerful," he said. "And the scene where you and your sister are arguing about who has the best marriage – man, you were so believable. I forgot for a moment that I was watching my daughter!"

I smiled and nodded and did my best not to look into his glowing face without being too obvious.

"And your relationship with your sister – it seemed so real," Meg said. "It really was amazing."

"You guys are too kind," I said.

"So, you have a cast party tonight," Meg said.

"Right, yeah, we're getting together at the Jazz Tavern."

"All right! Go have fun! We'll see you soon," Dad said, positively bubbling with enthusiasm. He hugged me again and then they were off, waving at me from the front door.

Of course, the truth was that no one was getting together. And now I was standing alone in the lobby holding two bouquets of flowers as some technicians drifted out, calling out "great show!" I imagined sitting in a booth with Alex, Dad and Meg, laughing and recalling the high moments of the play, answering their questions about various scenes and about the other actors. My eyes began to sting.

I set the flowers down on a table and texted Sam, asking if he wanted to meet me for a drink. But there was no reply. No beep. No chirp. Nothing. I drove home to that big empty house, put the flowers in vases and fixed myself a large drink to celebrate. And then another.

11.

Sam never did respond. Not even the next day. Some people were like that. Me, for instance. And I knew when I didn't reply, it was because I was avoiding someone – Alex, Tia, my dad, whoever – because I didn't want to have a conversation with them. So I could only suppose Sam didn't want to answer me the night before and that he saw no reason to do so now. Part of me was okay with that because if he was a bit of a cad, it helped me not to like him too much.

When I finally dragged myself off the couch and headed for the shower, I decided not to let it bother me. No big deal. If he was with friends the night before, or another woman, that was his business.

But when I reported to the theater that evening, he was the picture of affability, chatting in the women's dressing room with Melanie, Rachel and Helen.

"All right, ladies. Just wanted to tell you in person I'm

leaving town tomorrow morning, heading for my new job in Charlotte. The show was awesome last night. Didn't see any problems. No glitches. Nothing to fix. So, as the Lone Ranger always says: my work here is done. Just wanted to tell you what a pleasure it's been. And I hope we can work together again some time."

"Thanks, Sam," Rachel said. "Much success to you." And she gave him a hug.

Helen and Melanie hugged him too and echoed Rachel's warm wishes. I thought about hugging him, but held back.

"Yeah, thanks, Sam," I said. "I couldn't have done it without you."

And he took off for the men's dressing room.

The show was flawless that night, although I wasn't sure I gave as vibrant a performance as I had the first night. Maybe the audience didn't notice. We got another standing ovation.

When I made my way from the dressing room to the auditorium afterwards I was surprised to find Sam sitting in the front row.

"Took you long enough," he said.

"I didn't know you were waiting."

"Where's your car?"

He pulled my arm through his and we walked together to the parking lot beside the theater.

"Where to?" I asked.

"Your house."

I almost spoke a couple of times but couldn't think of the right thing to say. He was quiet as well. Even when we walked through the front door, he said nothing. He just wrapped his arms around me and kissed me for a long time. And then he took me by the hand, leading me upstairs to my mother's tidy bedroom.

"I hope you want me because I really, really want you," he said, pulling his shirt off. I finally got to see the tattoo on his arm – stylized comedy and tragedy masks, a symbol of the theater. If any tattoo might appeal to me, it should've been that one. But there was something about it that turned me off.

Still, as he undressed me, I realized I did want him. And I forgot everything else as we thrashed about. It was so liberating not to feel the regret, the guilt or the pain that had consumed my life. I felt so high, so free. It was like a drug.

And when we were done, he sighed and ran his fingers through my hair.

"You're coming to Charlotte," he whispered gruffly. "As soon as the show's over."

I swallowed and looked into his eyes, waiting for a visionsight experience, but nothing happened. We snuggled together and I drifted off, listening to him breathe.

When I awoke, I was alone. I couldn't figure out my feelings for Sam, nor his for me, but decided I didn't care. It was kind of like trying to figure out why you like steak. It just tastes good, even if it *is* bad for your heart.

That was the day my dad called and said he and Meg had some news they wanted to share and could they stop by for a short visit. I had just enough time to shower, dress and throw the comforter over the bed before the doorbell rang.

They were like young lovebirds, holding hands and exchanging looks with each other. They brought some homemade banana bread with them, knowing I would have nothing to offer, I guess. I did have coffee so I made a pot and we sat at the kitchen table.

"So you've got some news," I said.

"Yes," Dad said eagerly. "I'm guessing you might think we're crazy, though, because you think I'm so old. But…"

"Good grief, Tom," Meg said, chuckling. "You're not old."

"Jenna thinks I'm old."

"You're not old, Dad."

"Anyway," he went on, "we wanted you to be the first to know that Meg and I are going to have a baby!"

He looked from me to Meg and back to me again.

She smiled and patted her little baby bump.

"We didn't want to make an announcement until I was well into the second trimester," she explained. "I'm what the doctors call an elderly gravida. Which means I'm a woman of a certain age who's pregnant."

"Forty-three isn't that old these days," Dad said.

"Well, I ain't no spring chicken," she said, laughing.

And then they stopped talking and looked at me, waiting for my response. I was careful, as usual, to appear to look at them without actually meeting their gaze.

"I have to admit it's a big surprise," I said, "but I'm very happy for you. It's amazing after all these years that I'm gonna have a little brother."

Which gave Meg a start.

"Or a little sister," I added, trying to cover my mistake.

"Well, we had the testing done and it's a boy," she said. "So it *is* a little brother. How'd you know?"

I shrugged and laughed.

There was a lot of giggling and talk about a name, fixing up his room, buying a crib and a stroller and all that good stuff. I kept smiling even though I knew what the future held.

"Of course, this means you need to really take care of yourself, Dad."

"I do take care of myself. I'm an epidemiologist, for heaven's sake. I'm more than a little familiar with diseases."

"But I know you stay busy and I just want to make sure you get regular physicals."

"I do get regular physicals. Good grief!"

"Well, I know, but you need to be tested for cancer and heart disease and stuff like that too. You want to make sure you're around to raise your little boy."

"What a worry wart," he said, looking at Meg and shaking his head. "I told you she thinks I'm old." Then he gave me a defensive grin. "I'm in great shape. Hell, I ride my bike to and from work a couple times a week."

"And you've got the body to prove it," Meg said, squeezing his bicep playfully.

*

The show was sold out that night with a livewire

audience. And we fed off that energy. It was like I actually became Rose when I was on stage. We did two curtain calls afterwards to thunderous applause. I was flying high. So when I made my way through the house afterwards, I was unprepared for who was waiting for me.

"Jenna! You were wonderful!"

It was my teacher's assistant from school.

"Maria! Oh my God, thanks for coming," I cried, and hugged her.

"I knew you auditioned for the play so I watched for the ads," she said. "And sure enough, there you were with a starring role!"

She introduced me to her husband and their friends, who all told me how great the show was.

"So are you coming back in the fall?" she asked, taking me by surprise.

"No. No, I'm not. I've decided to focus on acting."

She nodded her head, looking disappointed.

"I ran into Daisy and her mom at the market a couple of weeks ago and she asked about you," she said. "She wanted to know if you'd be back."

Which made me feel guilty. But what was I supposed to say? She had no idea how painful teaching would be for me. Impossible, really. The kids deserved to have a teacher who could get to know them and care for them, not one who constantly averted her eyes. I just kind of shrugged.

Then I spotted Alex on the other side of the lobby. He was standing with Tia and another couple. It was obvious they were waiting to speak to me. But I really didn't want to talk with them.

As Maria and her group wandered off, Alex, Tia and their friends converged on me. I pasted a smile on my face.

"Congratulations," Tia said, giving me a quick hug. "Alex was right. It's a great play and you're, like, awesome."

"Thanks, Tia. I appreciate that."

That's when Alex stepped closer to her and wrapped his arm around her waist.

"Yeah," he said, "I told Tia what a good actress you are."

Even though I wasn't looking either of them in the eye, the mockery was impossible to ignore. I made quick work of my thank-yous and hurried for the door.

"Jenna!" Tia called after me.

I just waved and kept walking. I was absolutely steaming by the time I got to my car. And feeling an uncomfortable pang of jealousy. Why did I still want him? I had Sam. Alex was behind me. He was with Tia. I'd seen it. I knew it was coming. So why was I pissed?

When I got home I fixed my new favorite drink and checked for emails and texts. One from Tia, one from Dad and one from the genealogist, but nothing from Sam. Tia said she'd stop by tomorrow because she needed to talk with me about something. I texted her back, saying I had a doctor's appointment and then took my drink with me to the shower.

12.

It was with a great deal of irritation that I answered the damn doorbell, which wouldn't quit assaulting my eardrums no matter how tightly I pressed the cushion to my ear. At first I thought it was, like, seven in the morning or something. But when I opened the door, sunshine and heat slapped me in the face. I squinted into the brightness, trying to figure out whose silhouette I was staring at. When I saw the fake Michael Kors handbag, I knew it was Tia.

"Do you have any idea how shitty you look?" she said. "Even though it's, like, two o'clock on Sunday afternoon, I'd say you could use an injection of caffeine."

I let loose with a big yawn.

She brushed past me and made a beeline for the kitchen, rummaging through the cabinets while I made a pit stop in the bathroom. I splashed some water on my face, rinsed my mouth and combed my hair with my fingers before joining her in the kitchen.

She was making so much noise that I almost shushed her, but stopped myself just in time. I sat down at the table, feeling queasy.

"You got any food in this stately manor?" she asked, opening the fridge and more cabinets. "Well, let's see, a carton of skim milk, a box of Special K – woops, it's empty – a box of Triscuits and some disgusting cheese in a can. Hm. What will it be?"

She grabbed a small plate from the cabinet, laid four crackers on it and held the can above them.

"To cheese or not to cheese, that is the question," she said, waiting for my reply.

I shook my head and she set the can down and brought the plate of crackers to me. Then she poured me a cup of freshly brewed coffee and brought Splenda and the milk carton to the table, along with a spoon. I doctored the coffee as she started in on me.

"I had a visit from my brother the other night," she said, sitting down across from me. "You know, to hang out and play video games. Terry stopped at Mellow Mushroom and got a pizza on his way over. You know how I love Mellow Mushroom. Anyway, he didn't bring any beer with him, even though I specifically told him to bring a six pack. And so I was like, 'where's the beer, brother dear?' And he's like, 'we don't need beer with pizza.' And I was like 'oh yes we do.' And he was like 'nah, we can just drink Coke.' And I was like 'that's totally lame.' And I said 'you got money problems or something?' And he says no – that he just thinks we don't need to be drinking alcohol. Alcohol. He used the word alcohol. Mucho bizarro, wouldn't you say?"

I sipped my coffee.

"So my radar is on, if you know what I mean," she continued. "And I was like 'what's up with that?' And he hems and haws and tries to avoid the subject but I wouldn't let him off the hook, you know. And you'll never guess what he finally says to me."

I couldn't help it – I heaved a sigh and waited for her to continue.

"These were his exact words: 'Dad said he heard through the grapevine that you have a drinking problem.' That's what my big brother says to me, that my dad says he heard from *someone* that I've got an alcohol problem. Hell, maybe *someone* even told him I'm an alcoholic."

And she was quiet for a moment as I rubbed my eyes. But she wasn't through with me yet.

"So naturally I wonder who's been saying bad things like that to my father."

I could feel her eyes boring into me but I just studied my coffee cup.

"Are you even listening to me?" she asked.

"Yes."

"Well?"

"Well what?"

"Well, what the hell did you say to my dad?" she yelled.

My hands flew to my ears. The noise was like a hammer on my brain.

"I know you and Dad met at Starbucks," she spat.

"I was just asking him about a genealogist."

"Liar!"

"I'm not lying."

"Genealogist!" She jumped up, striding to the sink and looked out the window for a moment. Then she whirled around like she was about to shoot me.

"You don't need a genealogist! You need a psychiatrist. Because a screw has come loose somewhere inside your head. I'm like, really, really sorry about your mother, Jenna. And I wish you'd let me help you through the grieving process. But you won't even let me come near you. It's like you hate me. Normal people don't go crazy like this when their mother dies."

"Tia..."

"I thought you were my friend!" she whispered.

"I'm sorry."

There was a part of me that wanted to tell her everything. It would be such a relief to share my burden. But she was already telling me to see a shrink. I could only guess her reaction if I told her the truth. She'd probably go straight to my father and tell him I should be committed.

"Is that all you have to say?" she said.

I couldn't help it – I sighed again.

"Well, you know what?" she said. "That's not good enough. I don't care if you're sorry. Even if you really *are* sorry. It's a long way from making me feel better. You're nuts. And you know what else? You're mean! And you can sit here looking like a plate of reheated pork n' beans and wallow in all the self pity you can cook up in this great big empty kitchen. You can be Miss Holier Than Thou, if you want. I. Don't. Care."

She sailed past me and slammed the front door on her way out, causing something to crash to the floor in the living room. I wasn't sure what it was but it didn't matter. I just sat there staring into space, holding my coffee mug. I needed more than coffee, though. I also needed aspirin or something. But getting up and finding it was such a daunting prospect that I just folded my arms on the table and laid my head on them.

*

On my way to the playhouse Thursday evening I noticed my tank was nearly empty. That happened a lot lately and it ticked me off having to stop for gas when I was already running late. But I pulled into the QT, figuring I could at least get a few gallons right quick, only to discover it was crowded. Then I saw a pump open up behind me. So I popped it into Reverse and backed into the space before anyone could beat me to it. And then – boom! Some idiot bumped me from behind. I slammed it into Park and jumped out.

"What the hell!" I shouted as the guy pulled his car back a few feet. My rear bumper was crunched. And then he was standing next to me.

"Jesus Christ!" I barked, turning toward him. "You…"

And I was looking straight into a pair of green eyes that belonged to my father. And before I could look away, I stumbled backwards as the vision hit me. There was a scene of him helping Meg with her breathing during childbirth; them holding their baby boy; taking him to the park; helping him blow out birthday candles; sitting on the sand at the beach watching Meg and the little boy build a castle; Meg helping Dad get out of a hospital bed; then Dad was bicycling on streets filled with traffic. Lots of traffic. And a car sideswiped him, sending him hurtling through the air. And then – blackness.

I came to with my hands over my face, moaning. Dad was gripping my arms, holding me up. Then he wrapped his arms around me.

"Jenna, it's okay, it's okay."

He thought I was upset about the accident. I took some deep breaths, trying to get oxygen to my brain.

"Just some cosmetic damage," he said. "Easily fixed."

"Dad, I'm sorry. I was in such a hurry, I didn't see you."

"I know, I know."

The front of his car was pretty banged up but he must've slammed on the brakes in time to avoid serious damage.

"Are you on your way to the…"

"Shit!" I pulled out my phone to check the time. "I'm late."

"But you still need gas," he said, fishing his wallet out of his pocket.

"I really have to go, Dad. I'm not that empty. I'll fill up tomorrow."

"You sure?"

"Yeah, gotta hurry. Talk with you later."

I jumped in my car, desperate to get away. But it was

hard to drive because I was trembling. I'd almost forgotten how weak I felt after one of those episodes. And what the hell was that bicycle thing about? I went over and over the vision in my mind and tried to remember every detail of what I'd seen with Meg.

I was twenty minutes late getting to the theater and had to rush to get my makeup done and get dressed.

"Are you all right?" Rachel asked.

"Yeah, I just had a fender bender on the way over so I'm, you know."

"Are you hurt?"

"Just a little rattled." And I gave her a weak smile.

For the first time that night, I forgot a line. It was during the scene where "my husband" and I argue about having kids. We were in the middle of the scene. Randall said his line: "you're the one who wanted kids, not me." He stared hard at me, but it didn't help. I was blank. So he said it again, circling me this time: "And you know it's true: you're the one who wanted kids, not me." And when he had his back to the audience he whispered: "We made that decision together..."

And I jumped in.

"We made that decision together. I certainly didn't ambush you."

I don't think the audience noticed. But still, I was ashamed of losing my concentration. After our curtain call I apologized to Randall as we left the stage. He gave me a sneering shrug.

Sam didn't answer when I tried his number. I hadn't

talked with him since he left. And I felt this need to talk with someone but couldn't think of anyone else to call. I hated the sense of foreboding that consumed my consciousness. So I headed home where I could fix myself a drink and send Mrs. Robertson an email. I needed to know what she'd found out about my dad's family.

But halfway home, I ran out of gas. I pounded the steering wheel, cursing myself for letting the tank get so low.

"You stupid idiot!" I screeched. "Moron! Dimwit!"

I couldn't call my dad, that's for sure. Not after running into him, quite literally, at the gas station. No way in hell would I call Tia. But it was nearly midnight – not the best time to walk a mile or so to the nearest gas station. I looked around. A short distance down the road was a tiny shopping center I'd driven by a thousand times. Post Office, hair salon, Chinese buffet and a bar called The Filling Station. I headed for the bar.

13.

It was a dive – dark, loud and grungy – with a pool table in the back, a big screen TV and an empty stage the size of a postage stamp. A country song was blaring through dusty, oversized speakers. I looked around like I was searching for a friend and then took the first seat at the bar and ordered a beer so I could consider my options.

I could call a cab to take me home. I could call a cab to take me to the gas station, although I didn't have a gas can. I could call a tow truck to take my car to the gas station but that would cost a bundle. I could walk the distance to the gas station and ask if they had a gas can and then walk all the way back to my car. I glanced at the door as though my friend might join me any minute now.

It seemed overwhelming. I drained my beer and ordered another. About that time a guy sitting at a table with some friends sauntered over and parked himself on the stool next to me. He was, like, forty, forty-five, with a paunch, thinning hair and a wide, red face.

"You been stood up?" he asked, giving me a friendly smile.

I pulled out my phone and made like I was checking messages.

"No. Just a little late."

"Name's Bud, like the beer," he said and chuckled like he used that line on every woman he met.

I glanced at the door again and then took a swig of my beer. I was going to have to make up my mind soon.

"Never seen you in here before," he said.

Not good, I thought, that this guy was flirting with me. I tapped out a message on my phone to the genealogist, asking her if we could meet. I was still annoyed Tia thought I was making it up.

"I usually go to bars for younger people."

Not sure why I said that, except I was hoping he'd get the idea that he was probably old enough to be my father.

"Well, you're here now," he said, laughing. And he called out to the bartender: "Hey, Ronnie, bring the little lady another! On me."

"No, thanks," I said.

"I insist," he said, leaning close enough so I could smell the alcohol and cigarettes on his breath. And that's when he put his big hand on my thigh.

Without thinking, I splashed my beer in his face, which came as quite a shock to him and to me. But we both got over the shock real quick. I called 9-1-1 as he came toward me, beer dripping from his nose.

"Uppity little bitch," he snarled.

"Stay away from me!" I shouted as I slid off my stool. And then into my phone I asked the dispatcher to send the police. "A middle-aged man is threatening me," I blurted when she asked what the problem was.

"Middle-aged?" Bud yelled. "Hey, Danny, she says I'm middle-aged. You believe that?"

And his buddies converged on the corner I'd backed into.

"Leave her alone," the bartender called out, moving quickly in our direction behind the bar. "She's just a kid."

"She ain't no kid," said Bud. "You served her beer. And that means she ain't no kid. And she was flirtin' with me."

"I don't flirt with old men."

God, why couldn't I keep my mouth shut?

"I think we need to teach the little lady here a lesson, don't you?" Bud said to his friends, who laughed in reply.

Panic bloomed in my gut as they moved closer. I wasn't sure if they were just trying to scare me or whether they might actually hurt me, but I broke my beer bottle on the wall and waved the jagged edge in their direction. Thankfully, that's when the door opened and two cops walked in. Bud and his pals backed off like they'd scalded their fingers on hot coals.

"Is there a problem?" the shorter officer asked, glancing at the men and then at me and my broken bottle.

"No," said Bud, "no problem at all."

"Miss," the officer said, "you wanna put that down?"

I did exactly as I was told, setting the jagged bottle on

the counter.

And then the short officer talked with me while the other one talked with Bud, his buddies and the bartender. The cop asked me what the hell I was doing in that bar all by myself, letting me know I was lucky he and his partner just happened to be close by. I explained about running out of gas and admitted I'd made a big mistake coming in here and ordering a beer. I didn't tell him I ordered two. He and his partner gave me a ride to the gas station where I bought a gas can and filled it up. Then they drove me back to my car and talked me through pouring the gas into my tank. After thanking them profusely and promising I'd stop and fill up first thing, I drove straight home, fixed myself a whiskey sour, watched a stupid reality show and crashed on the sofa.

Buzzing. Something was buzzing. Then it stopped. More buzzing. Why? I drifted back to sleep. Way too early. Then the buzzing again. I realized it was my phone vibrating on the coffee table.

"Hullo…"

"Jenna?"

Tia sounded angry.

"Hm?"

"Oh my God. You're not even up yet. Again. Do you know what time it is?"

But she didn't give me time to answer.

"I want you to know I had a very interesting visitor last night. You'll never guess who rang my doorbell."

My eyes were closed and I really didn't want to open

them.

"A cop," she said.

Which, I have to admit, did pique my interest.

"A very nice, and I have to admit, a very good-looking police officer asked me if you got home all right. And I was, like, in my robe, you know. It was almost one o'clock in the morning! So embarrassing. And I said, well, I didn't know because you didn't live here anymore. And he was, like, this was the address on your driver's license. And I was, like, well, she moved out recently. And he was like, can you tell me where she lives. And so I gave him your mother's address. Jenna, are you listening?

"Mm-hm."

"And I asked him what the problem was and he was a little vague and said he just wanted to make sure you got home all right. And then he was gone. So, what the hell was that all about?"

"I ran out of gas."

"Why do I not believe you?

"Tia, don't call me a liar again."

"I didn't call you a liar."

"Yes, you..."

"All right, I called you a liar last time, but Dad says you did ask him about a genealogist."

"Listen, I ran out of gas on my way home from the theater last night and a couple of cops helped me get some gas. I had no idea they'd check to see if I got home. I'm sorry they woke you up, okay?"

I wasn't about to tell her the whole story.

"I wasn't asleep," she said. "I had a... guest."

And then my phone was beeping.

"I've got another call," I said. "Later."

I hung up to answer the other call. It was Mrs. Robertson, her voice so cheery and loud that I had to hold the phone away from my ear.

"I've got time to meet with you if you can pick me up in an hour," she said. "I want to take you on a little field trip."

Miraculously, I was only five minutes late, after jumping in the shower, throwing on some capris and a top and stopping to get gas on the way. She slid onto the front seat beside me, a black leather briefcase hanging from her shoulder to match her black and white outfit.

"You know where the Decatur cemetery is?" she asked as she buckled her seatbelt.

"Sure."

"That's where we want to go."

"But my dad's family is buried at Northview."

"This is about your mother's family."

"But my mom was..."

"Cremated, I know."

I started to say something else but decided to zip it, even though it was my father's family history I was anxious to learn more about. I thought I'd made that clear when we first met but couldn't recall our conversation clearly. Still, after that grim vision I'd had of my dad the night before, I wasn't sure what I was hoping to find out anymore.

Twenty minutes later we were strolling between granite headstones. The humidity was high but the clouds were thick, so it was tolerable in the midday heat.

"Here we go," she said, stopping in front of a large tombstone after consulting notes on her phone.

The marker was engraved with two names, John William Kelly and Evelyn Mary Kelly. John was born in 1930 and died in 1981, Evelyn was born in 1939 and died in 1994.

"Your grandfather died in a car accident," she explained. "And your grandmother died young, just like your mother. Cause of death listed as a heart attack. Just like your mother."

She led me deeper into the cemetery until we were standing in front of another set of grave markers. They were older and more weather beaten.

"These are your great-grandparents. Your mother's mother's parents."

The headstones read: Thomas Richard Murphy and Alice Mae Murphy. Thomas was born in 1914 and died in 1989. Alice was born in 1919 and died in 1965.

"Notice a pattern?" she asked.

"Heart attack too?" I asked.

"I didn't find a cause of death. Now, where's the other one?" And she looked at her notes again. "Oh yes. This way."

She walked deeper into the cemetery until we were in a much older section with tombstones whose engravings were worn with time. She led me to a plot with two small markers.

"These are your great, great grandparents – Esco

Jonathan O'Donnell and Mary Grace O'Donnell. Esco born 1890, died 1958. Mary born 1899, died 1931."

"Of?"

"Committed suicide."

Which made me sad and scared at the same time.

"Because of the suicide, I wondered whether the other women who died young might've had some mental health issues," she said. "So I poked around a little and found out that your grandmother, Evelyn Kelly, was admitted to a psychiatric hospital in the 1980s after her husband died. Treated for depression. I couldn't find any evidence that your great grandmother had psychiatric problems, but if I keep looking, I might. Depends on whether you want me to spend any more time on that."

She slid her phone carefully into her purse.

I looked up at the clouds, wondering how far back the visionsight curse extended. Was it a genetic mutation that passed this infuriating gene along the matrilineal line? Fascinating. But not what I needed most to find out right now.

"Or," she continued, "I can trace your mother's patrilineal line. Or maybe you're more interested in having me spend time tracing the families back to Europe."

"I'm not sure what kind of focus I'm most interested in for my mom's side. But I'm keen to know more about this kind of stuff – you know, medical issues, diseases, things like that – about my Dad's side of the family."

Bottom line: was my dad a ticking time bomb?

14.

A shiny black pickup was parked in front of my house when I got home. And a man was sitting on the front porch in jeans, a faded blue tee shirt, sunglasses and a Braves baseball cap. He looked to be on my side of thirty. He stood up as I climbed out of the car and I guessed he was about six feet.

"Hello," he called. "I noticed your lawn needs some attention and wondered if you could use a yard man."

I looked around at what had always been a perfectly manicured lawn as far back as I could remember. I was stunned at what I saw. Knee-high grass, overgrown bushes and the flowers my mother had carefully tended were mostly dead. On top of that, there were bits of trash here and there that must've been blown by the wind. A plastic grocery bag dangled from a big holly bush at the corner of the house. Embarrassing. How could I not have noticed how shabby it looked? The neighbors never said a word.

Damn considerate, I thought, that they hadn't marched over to my door and demanded I clean up the joint. And then it occurred to me – maybe it was one of the neighbors who called the yard man.

I took off my shades and he did too. He had a friendly, down to earth look about him. Light freckles, short brown hair, fit looking – like he was used to physical labor.

"Brian Mitchell," he said, shaking my hand.

"Jenna Stevens."

He had a melodious voice that made me think he might be a singer.

"So…" he said.

"I'm ashamed to admit I hadn't even noticed, which must sound kind of pathetic." I could hardly get the words out of my mouth and I wasn't entirely sure he heard me.

"So you want me to…"

"Yes. Yes, I do. Thanks."

And I hurried up the steps, needing very much to get inside.

*

There was no way I could get out of going to the baby shower. So I put on a happy face and did my best to help out. It was hosted by Meg's sister at her suburban McMansion. Huge rooms, tall ceilings and no trees in the yard.

Her sister and mother were so excited Meg was finally having a baby. I heard them talking in the kitchen with one of Meg's old girlfriends about how they'd been afraid she wouldn't get to have kids at all, and what a shame it would be since they knew she'd be a great mom.

It wasn't a typical baby shower. Not only were most of the people there middle-aged, there were a lot of men too – co-workers of Meg's, co-workers of Dad's, friends, relatives and neighbors. Not at all like either of the baby showers I'd been to with young women comparing how long their labor lasted, how tough the birth had been and telling stories on their young husbands. No one tried to scare Meg about what labor would be like or how exhausted she'd be after the baby came. If anything, the guests seemed to avoid that kind of talk altogether, which made me think everyone else might be as concerned as I was about the age of the parents.

Except for my grandfather, who, I guess couldn't help himself. I heard him telling a couple of guests it would be a lot cheaper if they'd just wait for grandchildren, which might not be too far off. Grandma wagged her finger at him like he should keep his mouth shut and I cringed at the implication.

Dad and Meg were so busy visiting with everyone, they didn't have time to notice I was avoiding them, freshening up the hors d'oeuvres or folding empty gift bags. They oohed and aahed over the soft, blue hand-knitted baby blanket I gave them. It was a substitute, though, for what I really wanted to give them, which was health and long life.

Another difference was that at this baby shower, wine and champagne were served. Which suited me fine. I re-filled my glass several times in the kitchen.

When all the presents were finally unwrapped and I

finished making the list of gifts and gift-givers, I snuck out and headed home. I called Sam as I drove and he answered just as I was about to hang up.

"Hey, babe," he said.

"I've only got a week left before the show's over."

"I know."

"You still want me to come?"

"Sure. Yeah."

"You don't sound…"

"I want you to come," he said. "I'm casting you in *Steel Magnolias*. But we're in final rehearsals. *Funerals* opens Thursday. No time to talk. So, ciao for now!"

And that was it. I set the phone on the seat beside me. I still hadn't told anyone I was leaving. It was better if I waited till the last minute. Less time for people to try to dissuade me. Of course, who knows, maybe they'd be relieved to see me go.

*

The play had gotten good reviews and we were sold out for our last four shows. Standing ovations every night. No one missed a line. Everyone totally in character. Rachel said we were a well-oiled machine.

I had learned to gaze lovingly into Randall's eyes while thinking of how he was screwing his way through life with his young co-stars, never allowing myself to be completely absorbed in my character.

After our final curtain call, we all changed into party duds and gathered at Rachel's Midtown high-rise condo. Who knew she was rich? It was on the twenty-first floor and had a stunning view. Her husband, Ken, was a developer and I heard him talking about their other home in Colorado.

Everyone was there, actors, stage crew, managers, business office folks. Everyone but Sam, that is. Melanie brought a tall, handsome guy as her date. Justin, the guy who played her husband in the play, brought his boyfriend, who was also an actor. Helen was with her chubby, grey-haired husband. And Randall introduced his wife Wendy who was wearing a low-cut, royal blue cocktail dress, her ample cleavage on display. I tried to feel some sympathy for her, after having that tawdry vision with Randall. But she gave me the evil eye, which I guess shouldn't have surprised me since I got the part she wanted.

Rachel had hired a bartender for the occasion, who served up all manner of fancy cocktails. When I asked him to choose a drink for me, he looked at me for a moment and then whipped up what he called a Spicy Mangotini. He laughed when I returned a few minutes later for a second one. We were all enjoying ourselves chatting, taking in the view, recalling our favorite moments from the show and talking about upcoming auditions, when Randall's wife suddenly appeared in front of me.

I was half-way through my third drink, but she was obviously way ahead of me. She must've started before she got to the party because even I could see her eyes were glazed and her head wobbled like a bobble-head doll. Now that I was up close, I could also tell she was a little older than I thought that day in the lobby. And her breasts looked like they were about to explode from her dress at any moment.

"What do you think of the view?" she said, slipping her arm through mine like we were close friends and pulling me closer to the large windows.

"Makes me wish I was rich," I said.

When we were directly in front of the windows, taking in the lights of the Atlanta skyline, she whispered to me so no one else could hear.

"I saw the show, like, eight times."

"Wow."

"And I know you enjoyed pretending Randall was your husband. Kissing him every night, probably sticking your tongue down his throat, wrapping your arms around him, rubbing your body against his. And that's only what happened on stage!"

"What?" I blurted, trying to pull my arm free.

"I know all about you and Randall," she said, holding my arm tight against her. "And I just want you to know..."

"Randall and I never..."

"...that I carry a gun," she said.

"I don't even *like* your husband!"

And I jerked my arm free, dropping my glass, which shattered on the ceramic tile floor.

"You can't fool me. I know what's been going on," she said, her voice rising and her eyes bulging. "Always late getting home, smelling of alcohol and women's cologne, talking about Jenna this, Jenna that."

"I can assure you I would never have anything to do

with your husband," I whispered. "Not in a million years."

I whirled around and marched across the room as the guests turned to stare, including Melanie, whose eyes darted about like a driver caught doing sixty in a school zone. Randall disengaged from a small cluster of people and sprinted toward his wife, which meant we were on a collision course. While I was actually heading for the door to escape the extreme unpleasantness, my anger erupted when we both reached the middle of the room.

"Asshole!" I hissed, blocking his path. "You cheat on your wife and then use me as a decoy. Is that what you do every time? Trick your wife into thinking you're screwing Actress A when you're actually screwing Actress B?"

"You'll never get another part in this town," he said, his voice low and menacing.

I remembered then who I was talking to – the pampered son of one of Atlanta's wealthiest arts patrons. But I couldn't stop myself.

"Melanie, get your butt over here!" I said, using my stage voice. "I'm not taking the fall for you." I looked at Wendy then. "Here's the actress your husband's been screwing. Not me. But keep in mind – *he's* the one cheating on *you*. Also keep in mind he's a repeat offender."

No one said a word as I stalked out, although I did notice the bartender grinning as he wiped the bar with a white cloth.

15.

Sam had texted me the address but I was beginning to think my GPS was screwed up by the time I pulled onto Elizabeth Lane. Was there another street with the same name and I just had the wrong zip code? It was a rundown, old neighborhood just north of downtown Charlotte. Lots of warehouses turned into apartment buildings, refurbished old wooden houses, big trees and people walking along the sidewalks. I parked and double-checked the address, looking across the street at a duplex painted aqua with a pink crepe myrtle in front. 213A and 213B had separate entrances on either end. A large oak shaded the small front yard. I rolled down my windows, turned off the engine and sat there. Rock music was blaring from somewhere. And the aroma of ethnic food reminded me it was supper time and I was hungry. I rolled up the windows and got out, locking the car as I strolled toward 213B.

Tapping on the door brought no answer. I knocked

again. Nothing. I texted him. No reply. I called his cell phone. Voicemail answered. I reluctantly left a message. "I'm standing outside your door. At least I think it's your door."

When I talked with him just before leaving home, he said he'd be here, that we could have dinner together. So maybe he was on his way home. I sat on the porch steps and waited. Which was fine, really. Maybe it would help calm my nerves. The closer I got to Charlotte, the more uncertain I'd become. Was I doing the right thing? But was there a right thing? I didn't know anymore. As I sat there on the hard concrete, it occurred to me that I could just jump back in my car and take off. I could head back down I-85 if I wanted to or I could drive east all the way to the beach. What the hell. But, of course, this was a good opportunity for me, getting another acting job so quickly. It might lead to bigger and better things. And there was something about Sam that I found... what? Stimulating? Plus, there was the added bonus of not being constantly on edge about having a vision.

About thirty minutes later I heard someone call my name. And there he was, jogging straight for me, grinning. He was dressed in baggy shorts and a blue polo, his dark hair longer and shaggier than the last time I'd seen him, which made him look sexy. He closed the distance between us and pulled me into an embrace and kissed me. It was not just a quick hello kiss either.

"Welcome, gorgeous," he finally said, leading me up the steps. He unlocked the door and ushered me into a messy living room, two beer bottles on the coffee table, clothes draped on a chair. "Come on," he said, taking my hand again and drawing me through the hallway to a bedroom. "This is yours," he explained, then flipped a pale green bedspread down. "Let's break it in."

"Sam…"

But he kissed me again and began unbuttoning my shirt.

"Sam…" I protested.

But there was no resisting him.

*

"What do you mean, I have to audition?" I asked.

"It's just a formality."

We'd walked from the apartment to an Ethiopian restaurant around the corner called Desta, which Sam explained meant "happiness."

"But I thought I'd already been cast."

"You have, you have. Wipe that furrow from your brow," he said, scooping his food with his flatbread.

"Annelle?"

"Shelby."

"I thought you said you wanted me for the role of Annelle."

"Well, at first I did. But this other girl auditioned and she was just perfect for Annelle. So you get the lead role. You're not complaining, are you?"

"Shelby," I said, and sipped my wine. Shelby was the character the play was centered around – the one who had diabetes, got married, had a baby and then died. It was a big role. A meaty role. It would look great on my resume.

"You come in tomorrow afternoon, you run through some lines and I make my choice official. Simple as that."

He scooped up more of his Fish Tibs and pumped his eyebrows at me.

*

The Lyric Theatre was only about five blocks from the apartment in a converted brick elementary school from the 1940s, along with some non-profit organizations and a little art gallery. The stage itself was on the floor, with seats rising from it in a semi-circle. No curtains. No proscenium. Very intimate.

Two caskets sat at odd angles onstage, along with several flower arrangements and a small church pew. *Funerals* would wrap up the week before *Steel Magnolias* opened.

"You'll love the set design for *Magnolias*," he said, ushering me to the stage. "Pink. Lots of pink."

"Do we have to use fakey southern accents?"

"Realistic southern accents would be better."

"And do I have to wear big 1980s hair?"

He laughed loudly and called out to someone sitting in the third row.

"Barbara, this is Jenna. Jenna, this is Barbara McLeod, founder of the Lyric. She's directed a lot of plays on this stage and acted in a good many of them too. And she's the one who hired me as Artistic Director."

She was a slender woman with short, silver hair, rectangular purple glasses and a matching purple outfit.

Probably about seventy.

"So this is the young actress you delayed auditions for," she said. "Better be worth it, Sam."

"Don't worry," he said.

"Nice to meet you," I said, smiling as friendly a smile as I could muster.

She ignored me, holding her phone to her ear.

"She's here," she said into the phone.

And then another woman appeared out of nowhere, tucking her own phone in her pocket.

"All righty then!" she bellowed, bounding onto the stage as Sam headed into the seats to sit beside Barbara.

"I'm Judy Phillips and you must be Jenna," she said, shaking my hand vigorously.

She was a little taller than me, at least thirty pounds heavier than me and old enough to be my mother. Her long brunette hair was pulled up into a loose, messy chignon, with strands of hair dangling around her face. Her red lipstick matched the red top she was wearing over a pair of tight jeans.

"I'm M'lynn," she explained, handing me a script and keeping one for herself. "We're doing the 'thirty minutes of wonderful' scene. Page..."

"I don't need the book."

She wagged her head and gave Sam and Barbara a skeptical look.

But I was ready. Sam had prepped me and I was a quick study. I turned away, closed my eyes and focused on all the frustration, confusion and pain I'd been feeling ever since my mother died. I thought of Dad, Meg, Tia and Alex. And I thought of little Daisy. I remembered all the depressing things I'd seen when I looked into their eyes. And I allowed myself to wallow in self-pity for a moment.

"Okay, let's go," Sam called out.

I faced Judy and nodded, keeping my eyes closed for a few more seconds. And then we ran the scene. I was feeling Shelby's urgent need to convince her mother to support her choice to have a baby, to support the choices she wanted to make for her own life. And when I came to the line that defined her character, about how she'd rather have a few minutes of joy than a mundane life, tears rolled down my cheeks.

Judy's eyes teared up looking into mine and then she hugged me.

"All right, all right, you get the part," Barbara called out, like she'd been hoping I'd fall flat on my face. Then she said something to Sam in a low voice and made a quick exit through the lobby.

Sam joined us on the stage, beaming with satisfaction.

"I told you, didn't I?" he said to Judy.

"Yeah, you told me, mister smartass. So, are we finally startin' rehearsals?"

"Tomorrow night, seven o'clock sharp."

"And don't you worry about Barbara," she said to me. "She played Clairee in the first production they did here way back whenever the hell it was, and then she directed another production of it ten, fifteen years ago, so she thinks she's the be-all, end-all authority, if you know what

I mean."

"Do you know you're missing an earring?" I said, pointing to her naked left ear.

"Shit," she said, grabbing her earlobes. "These are the sand dollar earrings Hank gave me." She looked around the stage for a moment and we did too. "Lordamercy. I coulda lost it at the mall, for all I know! Might have to go on eBay and find another pair so he won't know. Damn!" And she zoomed out the same way she came in, calling over her shoulder, "Hasta ya'll's vista!"

Sam grinned.

"She's a hoot," he said, nodding in her direction. "Always losing something. Now, let's go get some grub. What're you in the mood for?"

"Well..."

"How about the best pizza this side of Jersey!"

I smiled as he grabbed my hand, guiding me toward the exit. It was a nice moment of inclusion, warmth and triumph. But unlike Shelby, I was positive I didn't just want just "thirty minutes of wonderful." There had to be more to life than that.

16.

Heights had never bothered me. But then, I'd never climbed sixty feet in the air and crossed a flimsy, hanging footbridge before. And I'd never zoomed along a zipline or walked along a high wire from one tree to another. But that was Sam's idea of a fun date. Of course, he didn't tell me where we were going ahead of time. If he had, I would've told him no way. He kept me in the dark as we drove west of Charlotte to an eco-tourist park overrun with Scout troops, families and young couples who wanted to be outdoorsy without having to train, buy supplies or travel to actual wilderness areas without guides to babysit their every move. But even with those babysitters helping us along, I was nearly paralyzed with fear.

Sam said it would be a great way to spend our day off from rehearsals, which had become tiresome. It's not that the play was difficult or that my scenes were too challenging. It's that Barbara insisted on being there. And she had an opinion on every scene, sometimes every line. She wanted to talk about each character's feelings and motivations and back story. Judy said she was always like that, which is why the previous director left. I overheard Judy telling Sam one night as we were leaving our cramped rehearsal room that he should stand up to the "uppity old bitch" but he waved her off. Which meant rehearsals went on and on, and it took us forever to run our scenes. So getting away from it all was a good idea, although I would never have chosen a canopy tour.

"Come on!" he called out from the next platform.

Easy for him to say. He'd already traversed the swinging rope bridge, hardly pausing, unafraid of falling, unafraid of looking down.

"You do know you've got a harness on, right?" he shouted.

True, but we were so high off the ground, it was dizzying. I stepped gingerly onto the first step, grasping the vertical ropes that held the bridge up. Sadly, I wasn't the only one making the crossing. There was someone behind me and with each step he took, the whole contraption shimmied. Why had I let Sam talk me into this?

I forced myself to move forward, one step at a time. Unfortunately, I had to look down to find the next plank. I could feel the person behind me getting impatient with the slowpoke in front. Sam was laughing as he waited on the platform ahead of me. When I finally reached it, he pulled me to him, chuckling at my distress.

"God, you're so timid up here," he said. "And so gutsy

on the ground."

Just then a little girl reached the platform, looking proud of herself. She was maybe eight or ten years old. Unbelievable – that's who was behind me. Her mother clambered onto the platform a moment later and listened as her daughter raved about how much fun it was and how she almost fell at one point. It was a high-pitched blow by blow, delivered with maximum enthusiasm.

"You ready for the zipline?" Sam asked, pulling me around the tree trunk to the other side of the platform.

One of the guides attached the hook from the little girl's harness to the overhead wire and she leaped into the air, squealing with delight as she glided down the long wire to another platform in a distant tree. Her mother clapped her hands and hooted beside me, which only made my knees shake more. After the mom took off, Sam stepped forward.

"I'll go first," he said.

As he zoomed away from me, he leaned back for a moment, looking straight up into the branches above him, obviously soaking in the sensation of flying through the treetops.

We spent a couple of hours going from tree to tree on wires, ziplines and hanging bridges until my muscles were so sore I could hardly move. It's not that I was out of shape exactly, although I admit workouts were few and far between the last couple of months, but I was so tense, my muscles were in knots. At any rate, when we finally descended again to terra firma I struggled to keep Sam from noticing I was a little gimpy.

"Was that a blast or what?" he gushed as we took our seats at a riverside restaurant.

I laughed.

"Makes me want to do the real thing, you know?" he said. "A canopy tour in Costa Rica. Whaddya think?"

"Mm-hm. Definitely."

And he laughed, amused at my discomfort.

We had burgers and beer. Which helped, since I was starving. I ordered a second beer, the first one was so good. As we headed to the parking lot I thought maybe he should drive so I tossed him my keys.

"I'm not driving," he said, tossing them back.

"Well, I've had a couple of beers and …"

"I don't have a license."

"You let it expire?"

"I've never had a license." He shrugged and grinned. "I never learned how to drive."

I stopped walking and stared at him.

"And I have to admit it kind of scares me," he said.

"But you're so 'gutsy' up in the air."

"Good one. By the way, what's with that banged up bumper?"

I groaned at the memory of backing into Dad's car at the gas station. I kept meaning to have the damage repaired but couldn't seem to find the time.

I drove us home, considering the irony. Sam, the fearless one, the thrillseeker, was scared to drive a car. It was hard for me to imagine being fearful of driving. I didn't even think about it. My body seemed to drive the car automatically, my foot and leg adjusting the gas pedal and brake instinctively, my hands turning the steering wheel without my having to think about it. In fact, the car was like an extension of my body, which was an extension of my brain. How could a grown man be intimidated by driving? A man who was obviously not a timid person in any way.

"What's it like living in New York?" I asked.

"You'd love it. Lots to do. Always lots to do."

"And you take the subway everywhere?"

"Or the bus. Or Uber or Lyft. Or take a cab. You've heard of taxis, right?"

I chuckled.

"Seriously, you ever taken a cab?" he said.

"Of course, I've taken a cab."

"When?"

"Well... when I visited New York when I was in high school... from the airport to the hotel."

"Impressive."

I shot him the bird.

"So you want to get back to New York?" I said.

"Yep. Just building my resume, looking for opportunities. I'm flying up in a couple of weeks to meet someone at a theater in Brooklyn. It's what they call 'way the hell off Broadway.'" And he laughed.

"But you've only been here..."

"It's not a sure thing. I may be here a while. But if there's an opportunity in New York..."

My eyes were on the road but I could feel him watching me.

"Maybe you might wanna come too," he said.

Which was a scary thought.

*

The night of dress rehearsal, we were all a little nervous except for Sam. Barbara only stayed a few minutes because she had to go to some kind of gala. She made a few quick suggestions about our costumes and makeup and hurried off, wearing an expensive, sparkly black dress. It was a relief to see her go.

The scenes flowed nicely, I thought. We were all getting into character. I figured the opening night adrenaline would fill in the rest. Having an audience made all the difference for me. We ironed out a couple of minor kinks and wrapped up about 11:30 to applause and whistles from the front row. That's where Sam was sitting.

"I'd say we're ready," he said. "Great show, ladies!"

"Don't you call me no lady," Judy shot back. "No need insultin' me like that!"

Everyone laughed.

Sam and I were both in high spirits on our walk home. I was feeling the vibe of our little section of town – the music oozing from the country bar, the spicy aroma wafting from the Ethiopian restaurant and the conversation of people sitting at the outdoor tables as we walked by.

"You know what I'm hungry for?" he said, putting his hand on my waist.

"God, you're insatiable," I said, giggling as he kissed my neck and squeezed my butt.

As soon as we were inside the apartment he kissed me as he took my shirt off and dropped it on the floor, leading me to his bedroom. He unhooked my bra and tossed it to the other side of the room and tugged my pants down. Then he pulled me onto his bed, making quick work of his own clothes. It was like he was trying to consume me. It was not romantic lovemaking, that's for sure. And when he was finally spent, he threw himself on his back, panting.

"God, you are like a fresh, tree-ripened peach in July," he whispered.

I rose from the bed but winced when something on the floor poked the tender arch of my right foot. It was small and shiny, reflecting the light from the bedside lamp. I reached down and picked it up. It was a sand dollar earring.

17.

Hammering. I covered my ears but the thudding continued. It was Sam beating on my door. I forced my eyes open and squinted at the clock. It said 2:34 and I wondered what the hell he was doing waking me up in the middle of the night. But sunshine was filtering through the curtains and I realized it was 2:34 in the afternoon. He was shouting now, asking me if I was all right. I remembered locking my door when I came to bed because I didn't want him sneaking in my room while I was asleep. I'd brought the bourbon, the mixer and a glass with me.

"Jenna, I'm calling the paramedics if you don't answer me," he yelled, rattling the doorknob.

"I'm fine," I mumbled. But my voice caught in my throat. I tried again: "I'm okay."

"Well, unlock the damn door, how 'bout it?"

I sat up slowly, knowing my head would swim. And it did. As much as I didn't want to, I was going to have to make a dash for the bathroom. I pulled on my blue kimono and opened the door, not bothering to look at him as I hurried to the john. I threw up first, peed second, brushed my teeth third and then took a long shower.

My emotions were all jumbled. I cared and I didn't care. Part of me was jealous. Finding Judy's earring in Sam's bedroom infuriated me. It was kind of like discovering a revolting worm in a juicy apple when you were halfway through eating it. And imagining them together on the same bed made me feel low class. Had they continued having sex after I got here? On the other hand, why should I care? One of the things that drew me to him, ironically, was that I didn't love him. And every time I felt like I might be leaning in that direction, something happened to help me maintain my emotional distance. I never had to worry about seeing his future when I looked in his eyes. And it was a relief being able to talk with him and look at him. But there was a part of me that wanted to love him. Or, at least, wanted to love *someone*, to have an emotional connection with someone who loved *me*. I missed having someone truly care for me. Because I wasn't sure how Sam felt. He liked being with me. And he sure as hell liked having sex with me. He told me I was a good actress and even talked about taking me with him to New York. And sometimes that was enough. But sometimes, like right now, I craved so much more.

*

Peeking through the peephole before the show, I could see lots of grey hair in the audience. Which made me think

Barbara might be onto something in her eclectic choices – something for everyone. Probably helped with donations and support. The next show was a bittersweet, offbeat comedy. Sam said I should audition for the role of the Goth girl who falls for a teenage Elvis impersonator.

I'd gotten into costume and makeup quickly, fixing my long wig so the brown locks hung on my shoulders. I positioned myself at the other end of the dressing room from Judy. Suddenly, she wasn't funny anymore. Her homespun, country girl persona now seemed like a total put-on. I hadn't decided what to do with her earring. Maybe it was better not to mention it at all. Like she said, she could get another pair so she wouldn't have to tell her husband she'd lost it while screwing her young director.

I'd met her husband and he seemed to adore her. He was pushing fifty, a little paunch, but not bad, greying hair at the temples and a handsome face. He was a high school math teacher. I don't know why I found that odd, but I did. Of course, appearances can be deceiving. Who knew? Maybe he cheated too.

"Whatcha doin'?" Judy whispered behind me.

"Just wanted to see if we're sold out for opening night."

"Lord, yes. Barbara's been braggin' all week," she said, chuckling softly.

We still had a few minutes before Barbara took center stage to give her welcome speech. Sam warned me she stretched it out a bit longer than necessary because she missed the limelight and the applause. So I headed backstage, Judy right behind me.

"Nervous?" she asked.

"Just going over my lines."

She took the hint and left me pacing in the wings. I was trying to concentrate but all I could think about was Judy and Sam in bed. I wished I'd never found the damn earring.

Barbara's speech did drag on but the audience applauded when she was done, probably thankful the show would finally begin. Fortunately, it began with Truvy and Annelle onstage. And then we were zooming through our scenes. The grey-haired ladies and their husbands laughed and cried on cue. They knew the story. They knew I was going to die and they were ready to grieve along with my stage mother, M'lynn. Because I wasn't in the last scene, I watched from the wings as Judy broke down and wept for her dead daughter. She was totally in character and very believable. And I could hear sniffles from the audience.

There was a standing ovation as we all held hands and took our bows. And when we dashed off stage Judy hugged me close and then hugged all the other actresses and wrapped her arms around Sam and hugged him too. She was flying.

"Strong opening night performance," Sam said. "I do have a few notes to give everyone, though. I'll start with you, Truvy."

The rest of us wandered back to the dressing room while Sam talked with Vera, the plump actress who played the owner of the hair salon. He talked briefly with each of us, saving me for last.

"Any major problems?" I asked as we started for home.

"Your Shelby seemed a little too angry."

"Sorry."

"Yeah, you want the audience to like your character, to be sympathetic with your character."

I grunted softly.

"Maybe you were just too hung over," he said.

I wanted to defend myself but bit my tongue. I probably *was* too hung over. And too distracted. But his criticism stung and I took it to heart, determined to throw myself totally into being Shelby, wanting to have a baby with my wonderful husband, wanting to have a full life even though I needed a kidney transplant from my mother. I would force myself to think of Judy as my mother, my interfering, but well-meaning mother who was trying to save my life.

"You're an awesome actress," he whispered, taking my hand in his. "I think that's one of the reasons you turn me on."

As soon as we were inside the apartment, he slipped his hands under my shirt and kissed me.

"I'm going to bed," I said.

"Mm."

"Alone. I'm beat."

He looked into my eyes as though trying to gauge whether I was telling the truth. And then he gave me a peck on the lips and let me go.

*

I had no clue until I was leaving the theater the next night that Alex and Tia were in the audience. It was probably a good thing, because if I'd known, I would've been nervous. But when I exited the dressing room, there they were standing in the hallway. I was so taken by surprise that I almost looked them in the eye, but caught myself just in time.

"Oh my God," I said. "I can't believe you guys drove all the way to Charlotte to see the play."

"You were, like, wow," Tia said, giving me a quick hug.

"Yeah, really great," said Alex, although his level of enthusiasm wasn't anywhere near what it was the last time he came to see me in a play.

And that's when Sam arrived to walk me home. I introduced them. Tia and Alex praised the show again, congratulating Sam as the director. He was charming and gracious and relished the attention.

"Maybe we can go for a drink," Tia suggested.

Before I could think of a way to politely decline, since they had, after all, driven all the way from Atlanta, Sam agreed heartily and said he knew of a nice bar close by. Tia and Alex exchanged glances as though they were surprised Sam would join us. Of course, I didn't want them to know Sam and I were living together, especially Alex. But Sam didn't know that and he reached for my hand as we headed out. I dropped my purse to avoid holding hands, but it was too late. The jig was up.

We took a booth at Barney's, Sam sitting next to me. Tia ordered red wine and Alex ordered a whiskey sour. Was he mocking me? So when it came my turn I asked for a glass of Chardonnay and Sam ordered sangria and some snacks. It was awkward small talk till the drinks arrived.

And then it got worse.

"Didn't you direct the other play Jenna was in?" Alex asked, nodding his head at Sam.

"Yep. That's where we met. She's quite an actress," he replied, smiling at me a little too warmly.

"You can say that again," Alex said, gulping his drink down and raising his hand for our waitress to bring him another.

"How'd you get the role here in Charlotte?" Tia asked.

"Sam encouraged me to audition."

"Where you staying while you're here?" she asked.

"With me," Sam said, just as the waitress set Alex's drink in front of him.

"Anyone else ready for another one?" the waitress asked, looking at each of us in turn. Tia and Sam shook their heads but I nodded and pointed to my wine glass.

Alex took a swig of his drink.

"Yeah," Sam continued, "I rented a two-bedroom apartment so we're sharing the rent. It's just a few blocks from here. Easy walking distance."

Of course, if I'd ever told him anything about my past it might've occurred to him not to tell my best friend and my former boyfriend that we were living together. But I'd never told him any of it. He thought they were a couple I'd been friends with back home and it never crossed his mind to keep a secret anyway. Unless it was about the other women he was making it with.

Alex guzzled the rest of his drink and asked for a third when the waitress set my glass of wine on the table.

"You the designated driver?" Sam asked Tia, smiling.

"Guess so," she said, giving me a meaningful look.

It was all seriously uncomfortable and I was trying to figure out whether there was anything I could say to make it less so, but nothing came to mind. Sam talked about the neighborhood, which he said reminded him a little bit of New York. He talked about the next play he was doing, telling them he'd already encouraged me to audition for one of the parts.

"So, that's how you get your roles," Alex said. "On the casting couch."

His words cut to the bone and I looked into his dark eyes, which were glazed from the alcohol. Dizziness overcame me and I felt like I was falling as swirling images flashed before me: Alex and Tia in bed together; then the two of them having angry words and Tia storming out; Alex and a pretty woman with long, black hair kissing; then she was having a baby and Alex was anchoring the evening news.

When I came to, my wine glass had been knocked over and the liquid was spilling from the table onto my lap. Sam blotted my pants with a cocktail napkin as Alex gulped the last of his drink and nudged Tia to get up. He threw some bills on the table and they were gone.

18.

It took me longer to get from Charlotte to Atlanta than it should have because my car wouldn't crank after I stopped for a Frappuccino in Greenville. At nine o'clock on a Sunday night, I knew my chances of getting the car fixed were slim to none. But this nice man who reminded me a lot of Tia's dad said I had a dead battery and gave me a jump, warning me not to turn off my engine until I got home. So I scooted on down I-85, dropped my car at the battery store and took Uber to the house.

I was relieved when I finally walked through the door. At least I think I was relieved. The house felt like a museum compared with the Charlotte duplex. It was big, quiet and empty. I'd come home to sort out my feelings and to get away from Sam for a few days. I left after the Sunday matinee, telling him I had to take care of a few things and I'd be back in time for Wednesday evening's auditions for *End Days*. His reaction was matter-of-fact. No objection.

All smiles. Never said he'd miss me.

I had a couple of drinks sitting in my shorty pajamas in front of the TV. I chose a sappy romance to watch and fell asleep on the sofa, dreaming about a dark-haired man who gazed deeply into my eyes before kissing me.

*

The noise of someone breaking into the house woke me with a terrible start. I grabbed my phone to dial 911. But through the window I noticed a police car in the driveway. And I heard what sounded like a police radio – definitely voices coming from the back of the house. I ran to the kitchen and peered through the window. An officer was standing in the garden, his back to me. He was holding something in his hand, possibly a gun. I threw the door open and he spun around, reaching for his holster.

"Jenna!"

It was Brian, my new yard man. Only he was wearing a dark blue police uniform, a badge on his chest, and a gun and handcuffs on his waist.

"I didn't know you were home," he said.

He was watering the tomato plants with the hose. I opened my mouth but couldn't figure out what to ask first. I stood there for a moment, squinting in the bright sunshine, my head pounding, realizing I was dressed only in my PJs. Finally, I closed my eyes and shut the door again.

In the bathroom, I stared at my reflection. My hair was a tangled mess. There were dark circles under my eyes. And I think it would be putting it mildly to say I looked a lot older than my age at that moment. So I took a shower, letting the warm water pummel my neck and back while I tried to make sense of what just happened.

My car was ready to pick up, but retrieving it seemed like way too much work. I ordered Chinese take-out. I did have enough energy to get dressed before the delivery guy got there.

I checked my messages and emails while I ate and found one from Brian apologizing for frightening me. He said he'd drop by around seven, if that was convenient, to explain. And precisely at seven o'clock, the doorbell rang. He was standing on my front porch in jeans and a tan tee shirt, looking more like a yard man. In one hand there was a baking dish in an insulated carry bag, in the other, a gallon jug.

"Homemade lasagna and lemonade," he said, giving me a lop-sided grin.

I nodded for him to come in and he followed me to the kitchen.

"You made lasagna… all by yourself?"

"I like to cook."

"And lemonade?"

"Fresh squeezed. Perfect with lasagna. You'll see."

I filled two glasses with ice and poured the lemonade.

"I'm adding bourbon to mine," I said. "You want some?"

He shook his head.

"Can we eat on the patio?" he said, scooping lasagna onto the plates.

We sat in the cushioned chairs at the white table my mother had bought years before. I have to admit, I was a little leery of his lasagna but it was quite good, with spinach, zucchini, mushrooms, onions and lots of cheese.

"Don't tell me," I said after my first bite. "You also work as a part-time chef at an Italian restaurant."

He laughed, pleased by the compliment. Apparently, the homemade dinner was an apology for scaring me, but it occurred to me that maybe I should apologize for scaring *him*. It made me cringe to think how atrocious I looked when I yanked the door open and found him in my back yard.

"Where's your car?" he asked.

"I dropped it off when I got into town last night to get a new battery."

"Your battery died on the way home from Charlotte?"

I nodded.

"You take a lot of chances in your car," he said, shaking his head.

I was trying to figure out what he was talking about when I had this inkling of understanding.

"So you're a cop." I said.

"Yeah. But I have my lawn business on the side. You know, a little extra income."

"And we met before."

"I thought you'd recognize me."

It all came back to me. The night I ran out of gas on my way home from the theater, two cops came to my rescue and drove me to the gas station. A shorter one who did all the talking and a taller one I didn't really notice in my distress. And Tia said a police officer came to her apartment asking if I'd gotten home. And didn't she say she'd given him my mom's address?

"You're the one…" I said.

"Who checked to see if you made it home that night. And then I saw how tall your grass was." And he chuckled.

I dashed inside to refill our glasses, adding more Jim Beam to mine. We talked about what he'd been doing in the garden. I told him how my mother was into gardening and shared her summer bounty with me. He explained that the cages around the tomato plants kept the squirrels out. I told him they were a lot more elaborate than what my mom used. He asked if I'd like to try one. While I wasn't exactly a tomato lover, I said sure. So he picked a big one – he called it a beefsteak – and washed it while I fixed myself a third drink. He sliced it and put it on two plates. We got forks and knives and took our places on the patio again.

He took a bite and closed his eyes like he was savoring an exquisite wine, then smiled and gestured for me to follow his lead. I cut a small piece and popped it in my mouth and was stunned at the vibrant flavor. I nodded in approval. It was so much better than the Roma tomatoes my mother favored. And the difference between this tomato and what you found at the grocery was like the difference between fake trees at the mall and an old growth forest.

"See?" he said. "Nothing like a homegrown, vine-ripened tomato."

I was very relaxed by then but kept having to slap mosquitoes away from my bare legs, so we moved inside.

He was about to leave, I think, until I poured myself another drink. And then he sat down across from me in the living room.

"How's the play going?" he asked.

"Good. Good."

"You don't sound overly enthusiastic."

"Oh, I'm enthusiastic. I'm playing the daughter who dies. Which is kind of bleak, but it's a great role."

"What do you do when you're not acting?"

"Until recently I was a teacher."

Suddenly, I had to stop talking.

"But not anymore?"

I shook my head.

"You miss it?" he asked.

I wanted him to stop asking questions because I didn't have any good answers.

"Why'd you stop teaching?"

"Because I couldn't stand knowing..." and I sighed in frustration.

"Knowing what?"

Even though I was on my fourth drink, I could see he was studying me, leaning forward, elbows on his knees. His gaze was so earnest, so concerned.

I opened my mouth to speak, but caught myself. Why would I reveal my secret to this, this... yard man/cop? I rubbed my eyes and lay down.

I didn't hear him tidy up the kitchen. I didn't feel him cover me with a throw. And I didn't hear him lock the door on his way out.

19.

Messages the next morning from Mrs. Robertson: "I'll see you at 3:00 in my office;" from Tia: "Why don't you answer your phone, idiot?" from Dad: "We're coming to see the Sunday matinee next weekend. Can't wait;" another one from Tia: "Call me, dammit!" and a text from Brian: "your key is by the tomato plant."

Oh yeah – Brian.

Maybe coffee would help. I fixed myself a cup and tried to remember all the things I'd said the night before. Jesus, he must think I'm a nutcase. But maybe he just thinks I was drunk. Anyway, who cares what he thinks.

It was a little after noon and I still had to get my car. I showered and dressed and then remembered my house key. I stepped out back and studied the caged tomato plants, noticing the large rocks on a board holding the netting in place. That's where he'd hidden my key – under the first rock.

There were three big plants laden with fruit in various stages of ripeness. A huge red tomato hung about waist high on the plant nearest me. My mouth watered, remembering the flavor from the night before. That could be my breakfast. I moved the stones and the board so I could lift the screen and reach inside. But the tomato wouldn't come off the bush. I held the vine firmly in one hand and tugged the tomato with the other, but still, it wouldn't budge. This must be why Mom kept several pairs of garden clippers handy. I hurried to the storage chest by the back door and found a pair of clippers perfect for the job. I was pleased with myself as I replaced the mesh, the board and the rocks, making sure everything was nice and snug so squirrels couldn't get inside. And I had to admit three thick slices of that succulent tomato with a little salt and pepper was one of the best meals I'd ever eaten.

I called a cab – Sam would be impressed – and picked up my car in time to make it to the genealogist's office, although I admit I was running on fumes. But I could fill up afterwards.

*

"All righty," she said. "I've done some research on your father's side but I didn't find any pattern of medical problems, diseases, mental issues – anything like that. Some lived into very old age, some died in accidents or outbreaks of flu, and so forth. Your father's great-grandmother on his father's side died of a heart attack. And several of his ancestors on his mother's side died from tuberculosis. But a lot of people did back then."

"What about cancer?"

"Cancer? I didn't find any specific mention of cancer, although, who knows, some of them might've had cancer and been diagnosed with other diseases or died from something else before cancer killed them."

I was silent for a moment, staring into space.

"Do you want me to continue my research along that line or should I move on to tracing the family back to Europe?"

Disappointment must've been written all over my face.

"I'm sorry I didn't find what you were looking for. You're thinking your dad's family might have a history of cancer?"

I closed my eyes, trying to think.

"Does your father have cancer?" she asked.

"No."

She scrunched her eyebrows like she was trying to solve a mystery. But I didn't want to explain further.

"So," she said, glancing at the clock on her desk, "how do you want me to proceed?"

I didn't know whether I wanted her to proceed at all.

"Can I think about it and get back to you?" I asked.

"Of course."

*

Once I was ensconced at Panera and had finished my bagel, I braced myself to call Tia.

"About damn time," she said. "I'm sick of you not answering your phone and not answering my messages."

I took a sip of my coffee.

"Where are you?" she asked.

"Panera."

"You alone?"

"Yeah."

"Well, all I can say is what an asshole your director boyfriend is."

"He's not…"

"Oh yes he is. I mean, throwing it in Alex's face like that! I told him it was a bad idea driving up there. I was like, you need to just move on. And he was like, I just wanna support her – how did he put it? – 'support her artistic endeavors,' or something like that. God!"

"Alex is a nice guy."

"Tell me about it! And you dumped him. For no good reason. Just left him in the dust. I'm beginning to wonder if Alex is right – maybe you *are* using the casting couch to…"

"I am not!"

"Of course, Alex felt really bad about letting loose on you. He was like, I shouldn't have said those things. And I was like, au contraire, she deserved it."

"Is that why you wanted to talk to me? So you could make all kinds of accusations?"

"I…"

"And, oh, by the way, all that bullshit about you and Alex just being friends…"

"We *were* just friends until you totally pushed him away and broke his heart."

"And then you…"

"Don't you accuse me of…"

But I clicked 'end' and the call was over. I turned the phone off before it could ring or ding or vibrate again. I noticed then that everyone was staring at me, their looks ranging from amusement to pity to embarrassment.

I had hoped to make a quick escape but when I jumped in my car it wouldn't crank. I looked at the gas gauge and the needle was on empty. Below empty, actually. But this time, my new gas can was in the trunk, just waiting for another attack of stupidity. I walked across the busy street, filled my can at QT, walked back, struggled to pour the gas in my tank, spilling nearly half of it on my shoe, and finally got my car started. It only took a few minutes to fill up at the pump and I wondered why I hadn't done it earlier. I was furious with myself and slammed the door as I climbed into the driver's seat, nearly smashing my hand in the process. I took several deep breaths before pulling into traffic, stopping at the liquor store and the supermarket on the way home.

After storing my few groceries, I fixed myself a drink. It was still hot outside but I strolled onto the back patio and sat down at the table. And that's when I noticed something amiss. Several tomatoes were lying on the ground inside the mesh fencing. Green ones, partially ripened ones and a red one. I hurried over and discovered it was more than just a few. There were at least a dozen lying about and they all had bite marks on them. And then I heard a skittering noise and saw to my horror that a squirrel was inside the enclosure.

"You little bastard! How'd you get in there?"

I examined the mesh carefully, walking around the outside of it. No opening of any kind. How had he gotten in? Every time I moved, the squirrel fled to another corner. He was trapped and scared out of his wits. I kept searching but couldn't find a breach. And then it dawned on me that I must've accidentally let him in when I lifted the mesh and went for the clippers to cut my tomato. As soon as I stepped away, he darted inside. And then I carefully replaced the screen, the board and the rocks so he couldn't get out. I caused his pain and suffering. And I caused the loss of those tomatoes that were no longer fit to eat. I don't know why, exactly, but I burst out crying.

Finally, I sat back down at the table and took a big swallow of my drink. I had to let him out of there before he destroyed the tomato plants. I rummaged through my mother's gardening chest and found a pair of gloves and forced myself to remove the three rocks and then the board. Then I grabbed the mesh and tossed it up onto the top of the enclosure, leaving the side of the cage open. I ran for the patio, cringing at the thought that the squirrel might run after me, crazy with panic. But he didn't move. He stayed absolutely still as I watched, sensing, I guess, that I was watching him.

"Okay, little dumbass, I'm going inside now. See me going inside?"

With my drink in my hand, I backed toward the kitchen door. Then I ran inside, dashing for the window above the sink. I watched intently, determined to close the mesh again as soon as he escaped. I was halfway through my second drink before deciding I should go outside and check. I forced myself to be brave and inspected the entire enclosure, finally concluding the varmint snuck out while I wasn't looking. I must've missed it while pouring that second drink. Maybe I should've retrieved the ruined tomatoes, but I couldn't bring myself to go inside the cage. So much for being "gutsy" on the ground. I closed it up nice and tight and went back in the house.

Part of me wanted to message Brian about what happened. But the other part – the part that won out – didn't want to admit my ineptitude right then. Why would I want to talk about my life being jinxed, scaring the shit out of a poor little squirrel, getting into a fight at a bar, running out of gas twice, sleeping with a guy I didn't love and abandoning people who cared for me. Jeez, the list was getting too long to keep up with. I fixed myself a third drink and settled in to watch a movie. But they all seemed stupid and superficial so I gave up and turned off the TV.

20.

My makeup was deep purple lipstick outlined in black, with thick black eyeliner and fake black eyelashes. I powdered my face to make it look pale. The black wig was long, with bangs and a bit of spikiness on top. With my skinny black jeans, lacy black, long-sleeved top and fake black fingernails, I thought I could pass for a Goth girl.

When I walked into the theater, I found Sam, Barbara and a gangly teen-aged boy dressed in a white sparkly Elvis costume standing onstage. They were talking about the play and didn't notice me until I'd almost reached the front of the house.

There was momentary confusion as though they were trying to figure out who I was.

"Oh my God," Sam said, a smile sprouting on his face.

I grinned and shrugged what I hoped was a girlish shrug.

Barbara studied me closely and then raised her right

eyebrow.

"Well, let's get on with it," she said, stepping around me so she could take her seat – third row, center.

Sam made the introductions.

"Jenna, this is Cameron. Cameron, this is Jenna. Okay, let's do it."

He dashed up the stairs to sit next to Barbara while Cameron and I turned into the weird 16 year olds, Rachel and Nelson, of *End Days*.

It was the scene where they kissed. Fortunately, it was written to be awkward because it was definitely awkward. It's the scene where I tell him I've read *A Brief History of Time,* which he gave me, and he's so excited that I like it and I end up grabbing his face and kissing him, not once, not twice, not three times, but four times. And he asks me if that means I like him and I say "maybe."

And when I said "maybe," Sam called out "Cut!" and came dashing onstage, beaming.

"Wow!" he said. "Cameron, you sounded like you really understood what you were talking about – all that stuff about the Hadron Collider and the Big Bang."

"I googled it," he replied, shrugging his shoulders like it was no big deal.

*

"He's the exact age of the character," Sam said.

"He looks thirteen," I replied.

We were walking home and I was conscious of the stares from people who really thought I was a Goth girl.

"Well, I've cast him as Nelson."

"But…"

"Jenna, there are some things I don't have control over."

"You're the director."

"Well, Barbara pays my salary."

"So you're required to cast her grandson, even if he looks thirteen and can't act his way out of a paper sack?"

"He'll be fine. He takes coaching pretty well."

We walked the rest of the way in silence, each with our own thoughts. But he reached for me and pulled me close once we were inside the apartment.

"I've never made it with a Goth girl before," he said, and kissed me.

"No Goth girls in your repertoire?"

"Nope. But there's always a first time." He had an amused look in his eyes. "You really could pass for a teen-age girl."

"I thought you preferred older women."

"I'm what you might call eclectic," he said, kissing me again.

I wiped the dark lipstick from his mouth. It made him look like a bruised apple.

*

He was gone when I got up the next morning, which was unusual. I took a power walk, showered and had coffee and strawberries for breakfast. I was tidying up when he got home around one. He made an unusual amount of noise as he fixed himself a sandwich.

"You want a sandwich?" he called to me from the kitchen.

"Don't think so."

"Well, can you sit with me while I eat?"

I came out of my bedroom and joined him at the small kitchen table.

"I'm not gonna beat around the bush," he said. "We've cast someone else as Rachel."

I just looked at him, trying to wrap my mind around this announcement.

"I'm sorry, Jenna. I wanted *you* but Barbara thinks you look too old next to Cameron."

I stared at his sandwich. For some reason, I thought the role was automatically mine. Maybe I hadn't thrown myself into it. Maybe I'd taken it for granted Sam would give me the part. So much for the casting couch. I almost asked if I could have another chance, a second audition. I felt sure I could prove to Barbara that I was capable of looking young enough beside her precious grandson. But I kept my mouth shut.

"It's no reflection on your acting chops," he said. "You were awesome. Very believable. This is all about Barbara."

I stood up and walked across the room to stand by the window. For some reason the oak tree in the front yard looked like a painting framed by the window casing. Too perfect to be real.

"Jenna," he said, following me and wrapping his arms around me from behind. Then he kissed my cheek.

"This'll give you time to get your head shot done, your web site up and running – all those things actors have to do nowadays. You can audition at other theaters. And I'm flying up to New York next week, interviewing at that Brooklyn theater I told you about. If I get the job, you're coming with me."

*

When I arrived in the dressing room that evening, Judy was gabbing a mile a minute.

"It's such a different character," she said. "But Sam says I can definitely play a Jesus freak." And she laughed loudly, oblivious to the feelings of the other actresses who probably tried out for the role as well. But she kept on and on, talking about how funny it would be doing scenes with Charlie Silverstein who'd been cast as Jesus. "Hilarious, ain't it, since he's Jewish!"

I began applying makeup, trying to remain calm. Sam never mentioned he'd chosen Judy for the role of the crazy mother in the next play. And before I knew it, I was rummaging through my purse.

"Oh, Judy," I said. "I found your missing earring."

I held the little sand dollar earring up for all to see. She strolled over and took it from me, turning it this way and that.

"Well, how about that!" she cried, giving us all a toothy grin. "I never thought I'd see it again. Thank you, darlin'."

"You want to know where I found it?"

"Well, as long as it wasn't in the toilet, I don't really care!"

And she laughed big and loud, retreating to her dressing table.

I was on the verge of telling her how I'd stepped on it as

I was climbing out of Sam's bed. My lips were actually parted and I wanted badly to say it. But I realized at the last second what it would sound like for the young woman everyone knew was sleeping with the director to accuse the older woman who was also sleeping with the director of having sex with him behind her back. Tacky. That's how it would sound. And I was thankful it dawned on me in the nick of time. It was obvious Judy knew roughly where I'd found it. So I decided that was enough.

The show went off without a hitch that night. Judy and I were both professionals, you might say, and didn't let the earring episode get in the way of a good performance. If anything, we both stepped up our game. Sam was unusually chatty on our walk home, talking about what a fantastic show it was, how awesome and believable the characters seemed, especially Shelby.

"Judy must've told you about the earring," I finally blurted.

At which point he reached over and took my hand in his.

"Listen, Jenna, she has nothing to do with us."

I refused to look at him.

"You're my main squeeze," he said, putting his arm around my shoulder and pulling me close as we walked.

"Just out of curiosity, how many 'squeezes' do you have?"

He laughed and kissed me.

"But the thing is – you don't care," he said.

I thought about that. I guess it was true. I'd never given

him the impression that I loved him and wanted him forever and ever. We enjoyed being together and one of the reasons for me was that I didn't love him, didn't have that strong emotional attachment. I could look him straight in the eye without worrying about what would happen. And he must've felt that, even if he didn't really understand why.

His eyes were as excited about life as ever. He was always focused on the future. He must at least like me a lot and enjoy my company enough to keep asking me to go with him to New York. And who knew what that might lead to. Connections were important. And knowing a director – even if he was only a director of a Brooklyn theater – would give me a leg up. So when we got home, I cooked eggs over easy and toast while he filled our glasses with white wine. And when we finished eating we adjourned to the bedroom and had each other for dessert.

21.

After the Sunday matinee, I hurried to change so I could meet Dad and Meg in the lobby. I was looking forward to being showered with praise, although once again I reminded myself not to look directly at them. It was a hard act to pull off. But as I reached the front of the stage I heard someone call my name. It was Brian, my yard man, and a young woman with short blonde hair.

"Brian! Wow! I can't believe you came all the way to Charlotte," I said.

I reached out to shake his hand.

"Jenna, this is my sister, Amy."

She was about my height and very pretty in a violet peasant dress.

"You were wonderful as Shelby," she said, taking my hand. "Even better than your role as the young Rose, I think."

"Thank you so much. That's awfully nice of you."

"It's hard to say one was better than the other," Brian argued.

"You saw both plays?" I asked, looking first at him and then his sister.

"Of course," she said.

"You look so familiar," I said. "Amy. I knew an Amy. Oh my God, you're Amy Mitchell!"

And I gave her a quick hug. She was a classmate from elementary and middle school although we'd gone to different high schools. I hadn't seen her since eighth grade, which seemed like a very long time ago. She appeared to be pleased I recognized her.

"So you're her brother!" I said to Brian, trying to figure out all the coincidences.

"Yeah, she's the one who took me to see the play in Atlanta."

"Well, when I read in the paper you had a starring role," she said, "I just had to get tickets. I remember when you played Wendy in *Peter Pan* in fifth grade. I was a little jealous of what a good actress you were. Anyway, I asked Brian to be my date. I was going to speak to you after the show that night but you had a crowd of people around you."

"So, what are *you* up to these days?" I asked.

"I'm in medical school."

"Holy crap!"

They both laughed.

That's when Dad poked his head into the auditorium. He waved and smiled and I waved back. He and Meg strolled down to join us in the aisle and I made the introductions. We invited Brian and Amy to join us for dinner since they'd come such a long way but they said they needed to get back to Atlanta because they both had to get up early. And they were out the door.

Dad and Meg took me to a seafood restaurant and we had a fun dinner. As expected, they went on and on about the play. Meg said she cried after my character died. I have to admit, it was so gratifying having them gush about my performance. Her tummy was getting bigger and we talked about how her morning sickness was pretty much gone and about decorating the baby's room.

And then I posed the question I couldn't stop myself from asking.

"So, Dad, have you scheduled a physical?"

"Why in the world are you nagging me about that?" he replied. "I'm not that old, Miss Smarty Pants."

And he looked at Meg for support.

"She's just trying to be helpful, Tom. It does make sense, when you think about it. I certainly had a lot of tests done before I got pregnant. And a bunch more since then! If I'm an elderly gravida, you're an elderly... what do you call an older expectant father?"

"An optimist," he said.

And we laughed and moved on.

*

It was raining when I dropped Sam off at the airport Monday morning – the kind of rain that makes the whole world dreary. When I got back to the apartment, I climbed back in bed. I'd decided to stay in Charlotte on my days off rather than driving home, thinking I'd take his advice and work on my website and maybe go shopping. But I mostly spent the two days he was gone watching movies I'd already seen. You know, the romantic ones where the man and the woman overcome whatever obstacles are in their way and fall in love before the credits roll.

Sam was positively exuberant when I picked him up Wednesday afternoon. He kissed me when he climbed in the car, smiling and giving me a thumbs up.

"I got the job!"

And he kissed me again.

"Well, congratulations. That's exciting news."

"It's my big break, my foot in the door."

"When do you leave?" I asked, pulling slowly away from the curb.

"Next week."

"What about…"

"I already talked with Barbara and she's got someone who can direct *End Days*. I can't wait for you to see the theater. It's so cool. And I've already got an apartment lined up. You'll love the neighborhood. Lots of restaurants and shops. And you'll never believe what our first play is."

I could feel his eyes on me as I pulled onto the freeway.

"*End Days*. They already scheduled it before the other guy left. Can you believe it? I hope you saved your Goth girl getup. You'll be awesome as Rachel. It's a juicy part. And there's no Barbara waiting up there to put her thumb on me. What a relief. The apartment's unfurnished so we'll have to buy some furniture. But I saw a couple of used furniture stores close by."

He rattled on all the way home. I don't think he even noticed I didn't say anything because all I had time to do was nod and smile. And when we walked through the front door he grabbed me up and whirled me around.

"Let's celebrate!" he said, his eyes big with excitement. "You got a dress you can wear tonight?"

He called some theater friends and told them to meet us at The Queen's Pub for dinner and drinks – that he had some news to share. Two hours later we were ordering our first round. There were six of us – Sam, me, a couple of theater guys he'd gotten to know, Sean and Jermaine, our young stage manager, Caitlyn, and, of course, Judy.

"What gives? What's your big news?" she asked.

She had on her usual uniform – tight jeans and a form-fitting, V-neck top to show off her cleavage. This one was bright yellow and she was wearing dangly seahorse earrings.

"The drinks aren't here yet," he replied with a devilish grin.

"Come on, Sam," said Caitlyn.

She was in her late twenties, plump with long blonde hair. Pretty, but her tight dress showed off every bulge. I suddenly found myself wondering if Sam had made it with her too.

Sean was an aspiring playwright. He was short and slight, with dark hair and a pale complexion. Jermaine was his actor boyfriend – a tall, handsome black man.

Our waitress zoomed in with our drinks and took our dinner order. And as soon as she was gone Sam raised his glass and looked around the table.

"I want to propose a toast," he said, "to myself!" Everyone laughed. "Because I've just been hired as Artistic Director of the Waverly Playhouse, a 'way the hell off Broadway' theater in Brooklyn, New York!"

"Woohoo!" Caitlyn cried, holding her glass in front of her.

"Very cool," said Sean.

"To the big shot!" said Judy.

We clinked our glasses together and then Sam launched into an animated description of his trip to New York, his interview, the theater, the neighborhood – everything he'd told me and then some.

"Can I come with you?" Caitlyn blurted.

"Yeah, Sam," said Judy. "You taking any of your posse?"

He winked and nodded his head at me.

"Well, ain't you the lucky one," Judy said, raising her daiquiri in my direction, bobbing her head from side to side. "A star is born."

Our food arrived then – huge, fancy hamburgers with sweet potato fries and onion rings – along with our second round of drinks. Everyone pigged out, got sloshed and made Sam the center of attention. It was obvious they were happy for him and probably also hoping he might turn out to be a good contact. Except for Judy, who seemed content to be a big fish in a small pond, rather than a little fish in a very large swamp. Her husband, Hank, arrived as we were working on our fourth drink. He pulled a chair over and sat close to his wife, putting his arm around her.

"Can I have some of your fries?" he asked, popping one in his mouth.

"You won't believe where Sam's headin' off to," she said to him. "The Big Apple!"

"No kidding," Hank said.

"Brooklyn, actually," Sam replied.

"Congrats," Hank said, "and good luck." Then he leaned closer to Judy, kissing her on the cheek. "You ready to go?"

"Yup," she said and drained her glass.

She laid several bills on the table and walked out with Hank's hand on her waist. They were talking and smiling as they headed out the door, obviously very comfortable with each other. They'd been married for twenty years, had three kids and still seemed like a happy couple.

*

Sam held my hand as we walked home but he'd finally tired of talking. When we turned the corner onto our street, he stopped and stood in front of me.

"I missed you," he said, leaning in for a kiss. "Did you miss me?"

"Mm-hm."

And he kissed me again.

"Jenna," he said, looking into my eyes, "you know I think I could love you if you loved me."

And his lips were on mine again.

"I've been waiting for you to tell me you love me," he whispered.

"I have to love you first?"

"Yeah, I think so."

But I couldn't say it because my heart didn't feel it. I didn't resist, though, when he led me into the deep shade beneath the huge oak in our front yard, which blocked the light from the street lamps. And I didn't resist when he lifted my dress and we did the deed right there, with my back against the massive tree trunk.

22.

Butterflies. I guess that's why I knocked my makeup kit off the dressing table, sending it crashing to the floor. My lipsticks, foundation, powder, eye makeup, blush and brushes scattered everywhere. As I bent down to pick up the mess I whacked my knee on the chair, crying out in pain and frustration.

"Well, damn, Jenna, are you all right?" Judy said as she hurried over.

I couldn't answer because I was clutching my knee and trying not to cry.

"Crystal, can you get some ice from the fridge?" she said to the girl who played Annelle.

I sat down carefully in the metal chair.

"You break the skin?" she asked me.

My eyes were clamped shut but I tried to relax and breathe.

"Let me see," she said.

"I'm fine," I muttered.

It was one thing to have her play my mother in the show, quite another to have her mother me in the dressing room.

Then Crystal rushed in with a ziplock bag full of ice cubes and handed it to Judy, who quickly wrapped it in a couple of paper towels.

"Here, this'll soothe it a bit," she said, passing the homemade ice pack to me.

I placed it on my knee, noticing there was no blood. It would be an ugly bruise, though.

Then Judy and Crystal cleaned up the mess on the floor, returning the usable makeup to my dressing table and sweeping the broken bits of plastic and makeup powder into a dust pan.

"You able to do the show?" Judy asked me.

I nodded.

"Sorry for all the drama," I said. "Especially before the final show."

Everyone laughed, except me.

So it was a challenge getting ready, finding the right tubes and compacts. I was still applying makeup when the others were getting into costume. I hurried to catch up, managing to exit the dressing room only a couple of minutes after the rest of them. But as I trotted backstage, Judy smirked at me.

"Your wig's on crooked," she said, and took it upon herself to straighten it.

"Judy!"

I was about to tell her to get her hands off me. It almost popped out of my mouth but I realized I needed to focus and breathe, not lose my temper. I waited till she finished, then put some distance between us so I could run my first few lines while I did some stretches.

"Full house," Crystal said happily.

The show opened with lots of energy. And I figured my distraction would subside as I got into character. I really felt like I was "on" when I cried real tears during that first scene in Truvy's hair salon when Shelby suffers from too much insulin and Judy, as my mother, forces me to drink orange juice to bring me back. Shelby's anger and pain were so intense to me at that moment. And when M'Lynn explained to the others that the doctor told me I couldn't have children, I was positively livid. How dare she talk about me like I wasn't even there, throwing cold water on my hopes! The anger made me feel hot and sweaty. And when I looked into Judy's eyes, as she was baby talking to me and pouring more juice down my gullet, I suddenly felt genuinely weak and disoriented. I didn't realize until the very last second that my worst nightmare was coming true – I was having a visionsight in front of a live audience.

The images flashed before me in quick succession, like a full-color silent movie. First, I saw Judy taking bow after bow as she got a standing ovation; then she was in bed with a younger man; then she was happily putting a huge dinner on the table for her family; next, there was a scene of her and her husband cooing to their first grandchild; then she was having sex with another guy young enough to be her son; and finally, she and Hank were celebrating their 50th wedding anniversary, slicing into a heart-shaped cake.

When I came to, Judy was holding my chin with one hand and pretending to pour juice in my mouth with the other. She was whispering to me but they weren't lines from the play.

"Jenna, you all right?"

The first thing I saw was her anxious face inches from mine. The rest of the cast crowded around as well, which was not the way the scene was blocked. It dawned on me they were forming a protective wall so no one could see me. Even though I was weak and couldn't yet think properly, I could feel unease from the house, like the audience was holding its breath.

"Shelby?" Judy whispered, still holding the glass to my mouth.

How long had I been out, I wondered, trying to force myself to the surface, like I had dived into the water only to become trapped on the bottom of a pond, my legs embedded in muck, too weak to free myself. The voices were muffled as though my ears were filled with water.

"Come on, Shelby," she whispered, a little louder this time, still holding my chin in her hand.

I took a deep breath, filling my lungs with air, scooted up in the chair and cleared my throat. Which seemed to trigger a slight murmuring in the audience as the other actresses backed away, finding their marks.

Then Judy said her line and nodded at me and I realized

where we were in the scene and I delivered my line, telling her not to talk about me in the third person like that. But I was shaky, unsteady. And my voice sounded as tremulous as an old woman's. And it was obvious she and the others were on pins and needles, wondering what the hell was going on. Thankfully, I was seated in the beautician's chair. I could only imagine what would've happened if I'd been standing. We made it through the scene and when the curtains finally closed, we rushed offstage as the stage crew hustled onto the set.

The rest of the show went smoothly although I could tell the cast had a collective case of nerves. Judy, Crystal and the others were keeping their eyes on me, just in case. But I figured that's exactly what my character, Shelby, had to endure – people watching her, waiting for her body to fail. So I used that defensiveness in my performance.

When we took our final bows, it was to roaring applause. I was the last one to dash onstage and when I did, the audience rose for a standing ovation. If we'd been a rock group, we would've had to do an encore. When it was finally over, I sprinted to the dressing room, flung my clothes and wig on the chair, pulled my own clothes on, grabbed my ruined makeup kit and rushed for the back door, trying desperately to slip away before anyone caught me. But I wasn't fast enough. Just as I was hurrying through the door Sam called my name.

"I'm going home," I called out, without slowing my pace. "See you later."

I double-timed it down the back steps and across the

parking lot to the sidewalk. But he ran after me, catching my arm and spinning me around.

"You're not skipping the cast party!"

"That's exactly what I'm doing."

"You're all anyone can talk about," he argued. "How you made the scene with the orange juice so realistic, we were all holding our breath. Even Barbara was impressed. You were on fire tonight."

"Not going."

"If you want to build a good reputation as an actress and not burn any bridges, you'll…"

"Listen, the last time I went to a cast party, that's exactly what I did: burn bridges."

He laughed, wrapping his arms around me.

"We won't stay long," he said. "Just let everyone fawn over you a bit and then we'll go home."

Did he really not know what happened? He was sitting next to Barbara for the show. Best seats in the house. Was he really unaware of my crisis?

"Why would you want to skip the cast party anyway?" he asked. "Everybody's waiting for you."

I took a deep breath.

By the time we arrived at Nathan's Tavern I'd regained my composure. If everyone thought my performance was brilliant, then I wouldn't try to disabuse them of that notion.

Cheering greeted us as we strolled in. Lots of hugs and congratulations. Sam got me a drink and showered me with praise. I'd just begun to relax when Barbara patted my arm.

"Kudos, dear. I don't think that scene has ever been portrayed with more realism."

I was about to say thank you but she didn't give me time.

"In fact, I thought for a moment you were actually having a fit of some kind. It looked so authentic."

"Well…" I said.

"Judy says she thought so too."

"A fit? Really?"

"Or a seizure of some kind."

Which sent a flutter through my stomach.

"Wow. It sounds like all the research I did on diabetic hypoglycemia paid off," I said, smiling.

Sam appeared by my side then, like my knight in shining armor, handing me another drink.

"Man oh man, what an amazing finale," he said, chuckling. "Don't you think so, Barbara?"

"Indeed."

Judy never said a word to me about it and Sam seemed clueless about her suspicions. Either that, or he was pretending. But later, as we were making our way to the exit and wishing everyone good luck, I heard Barbara's voice behind me saying "Well, I'm just glad the audience was fooled." I don't know if Sam heard or not.

He rattled on about the show on our walk home. I tried to listen but my mind was elsewhere. I knew everyone was already talking about me in the bar. Of course, they wanted me to come to the cast party. They wanted to look me over so they could figure out what kind of attack I'd had on stage. It's possible that bets had even been placed!

It totally pissed me off that I let it happen. And what I'd seen in Judy's eyes kept re-playing in my head. Family, love and happiness, with some younger men on the side. I didn't know what to make of her.

I think Sam sensed I was already miles away from him. At any rate, we each slept in our own beds and then hurried to pack up in the morning.

When I pulled over to the curb to let him out at the airport, he leaned across to kiss me good-bye.

"Already missing you," he said.

As I drove away, I noticed the sunlight had changed. It was that moment in mid-August when you get a preview of autumn even though it still gets into the nineties by late afternoon. But you know that summer is drawing to a close.

23.

It was nearly seven by the time I got to Atlanta. I stopped at Kroger before heading home. Had to put the groceries in the back seat because my trunk still wouldn't open. Maybe I could get my bumper fixed while I was home.

When I stepped through the front door I was overwhelmed once again with how deserted the house seemed, despite all the furniture, the curtains, the paintings. The rooms were big and sterile. There was nothing of me here. It was like I'd hired an interior decorator who had no clue what I liked. I wished I could call someone but couldn't figure out who.

I put the groceries away and hauled my suitcases in from the car. I set them in the foyer, not wanting to go upstairs. If I stayed downstairs, it felt more temporary. Which was good. I fixed myself a whiskey sour to go with a pre-packaged salad I'd bought and was just sitting down in front of the TV when my phone rang. It was Dad.

"So, no problems on the trip?"

"Totally uneventful."

"Good. Listen, you'll never guess who I ran into getting an oil change the other day."

"Who?"

"Louis Spencer. Got to talking with him and told him you'd be in town for a few weeks and he invited us over for dinner – you, me and Meg – this Friday night. I told him that sounded great."

"Nice," I said, although I was already trying to think of a way to get out of it.

"So mark your digital calendar – Friday, six o'clock. Of course, Meg wants you to come over here for dinner one night too. How's Wednesday evening?"

"Well, sure, I…"

"Great! See you Wednesday."

Dad sounded so happy. I could only guess they wanted to show me the baby's room.

I'd finished my salad and my second drink when the doorbell rang. I found Brian smiling at me on the front porch in shorts and a tee shirt.

"Didn't want to scare you again. Just dropped by to tend the garden."

"Of course. How's it going?"

"Very productive. Soil's good. Probably a lot of mulch in it. I'll walk around the house. Didn't mean to bother you."

"No bother. In fact, I'd like to see it. Come on through."

He followed me to the back door. It was still very warm outside even though the sun was setting. He attached the sprinkler to the hose and set it up. But before turning it on, he removed the fencing and picked four big ripe tomatoes and then replaced the wire.

"Two for you and two for me," he said.

"Good deal."

He proceeded to pick several bell peppers, setting them on the patio table. Then he checked some other plants along the side of the garden.

"Come take a look," he called.

I wandered out to where he was standing and was stunned to see several small watermelons.

"They're Garden Babies, for small spaces. This one's ready," he said, thumping the largest of them. "You like watermelon?"

"Sure," I lied, wanting to prolong his visit.

There was something about his voice that reminded me of my favorite freshly ground Brazilian coffee.

He broke the stem and carried the melon to the patio. Detaching the sprinkler from the hose, he washed the melon before setting up the sprinkler again.

"Want a slice?" he said.

"Why not?"

I dashed inside, got a long knife, three plates, a stack of napkins, and a couple of forks and knives. He sliced it open on one of the plates. It was bright red inside. He cut the halves again and put a slice on my plate and one on his. I took a small bite and it was perfectly sweet and juicy.

"Wow!" I said, wiping juice off my face with a napkin.

I ate the entire piece as he devoured the rest of the little melon.

"Best watermelon I've ever eaten," he said, patting his stomach.

I had to laugh, I don't know why.

"This is why I like gardening," he said. "Real food is good for the soul."

"Real food," I repeated, nodding my head. "By the way, thanks again for coming to see the play last week. I can't believe you and Amy drove all that way."

"It was worth it. And Amy's right, you're an awesome actress."

"I really appreciate that. Still, it was a long drive. And I was so surprised when I realized who she was. So she took you to see the Atlanta play before you and your partner rescued me that night?"

"Yeah. I knew who you were."

"So that's why you guys were so helpful."

"Well..."

"What did Amy tell you?"

"Just that you were a good person, that you were very kind to a couple of kids who didn't have any friends."

I tried to think back, to recall who she was talking about. There was Tia, of course. Yeah, Tia. She didn't have friends when she moved here. And for some reason, the other kids didn't like her. Thought she was snooty and smart-alecky. A couple of kids, he said. Who else? I remembered a girl named Olga who moved here from

Russia. She could hardly speak English and the other kids thought she was dorky. No one would invite her over. So I did. And we became good friends. I really missed her when she moved to California when her dad got a better job there.

"So how much older are you than Amy?"

"Four years. But she's the smart one."

I laughed.

"Well, I gotta go," he said. "I'm picking up a friend to go shoot some baskets."

He pulled a string bag from his pocket and put the produce in it, turned off the sprinkler and recoiled the hose while I cleaned up the table.

"Will you be home for a while?" he asked.

"Couple of weeks."

"And then?"

"Thinking I might head to New York."

He nodded.

"Well, is it okay if I stop by and do the yard work and gardening when I have the time?"

"Of course. I promise I won't call the cops." And I chuckled.

He waved as he walked around the corner of the house.

Nice guy, I thought. And, for some reason, I felt so at ease with him. Nice sister too. I tried to remember why Amy and I hadn't become friends. We'd been in the same classes some years. I remembered her in my second and third grade classes. Then again in fifth grade. In middle school we shared some classes too. But she had her peeps and I had mine.

*

"So you're going to follow this guy to New York?" Dad asked.

He was grilling salmon and veggie kebabs while Meg and I sat in patio chairs. She was drinking iced tea, I was drinking Chardonnay. We had already set the picnic table, which looked festive, as Meg put it, with a pink-checked tablecloth. Bowls of sliced peaches and potato salad were waiting in the fridge.

"He's got a part for me," I explained again. "It's a really great character."

"Are you sure about this guy?" Dad asked.

"Sure of what?"

He carefully rotated the skewers as small trails of savory smoke wafted skyward.

"I just mean – is he a good guy? Can you trust him?" Dad said.

I wasn't going to tell him about my own doubts, that I wasn't sure I wanted to stay with Sam, that I wasn't sure about someone who said I had to love him first before he loved me, that I wasn't sure about anything anymore. So all I said was "yes."

"I guess you need to buy some furniture when you get up there?" Meg asked.

"Thank you," I mouthed silently behind Dad's back.

The conversation shifted to more mundane things. But a short time later when we'd moved to the table and were enjoying our picnic supper, Dad mentioned seeing Mr.

Spencer.

"You know, when I saw Louis the other day, he told me you're working on a family history, that you asked him to recommend a genealogist. You didn't tell us about that."

"Well, I just wanted to find out more about my ancestors."

"Have you discovered anything interesting?"

"Well, I haven't gotten the genealogist's report yet but she's told me a few things. In fact, one day she walked with me through the Decatur cemetery showing me some head-stones of Mom's relatives."

"You know, that's a great idea, Tom," Meg said. "I'd love to have a family history done of my family. And maybe we could piggy-back onto Jenna's leg work on your side of the family. Wouldn't that be great to share with the next little bud on our family tree?"

She patted her belly and grinned.

He nodded enthusiastically as he heaped a second spoonful of potato salad on his plate.

Of course, that only made me nervous because the focus of my research was all about disease, not who begat whom.

The tour of the baby's room came after supper and before the ice cream. Meg and Dad were so proud of the nursery. The walls were baby blue with puffy white clouds painted on a pale blue ceiling. Adding to the effect was a cloud mobile above the crib. There was also a floor-to-ceiling tree decal in one corner so that it looked like a park in there. The furniture was white and there were touches of Winnie the Pooh.

Meg showed me tiny overalls, booties, toys, the high-tech baby monitor, the newborn diapers stacked neatly on the changing table and all kinds of other baby stuff. Her belly was getting big now and she was wearing actual maternity clothes. She glided over to stand next to Dad and they wrapped their arms around each other, both of them looking the picture of health and happiness. But I couldn't help wondering whether cancer cells were spreading through my dad's body at that very moment.

24.

Dinner at Mr. Spencer's was a potluck affair. Meg volunteered to bring baked, stuffed squash and blueberry peach cobbler. I told him I'd bring some to-die-for tomatoes from my garden, well, from Brian's garden, and I'd stop and get a nice bottle of wine on the way.

Looking at my reflection, I decided I was overdressed in black slacks and a silvery top. I changed into teal capris and a pale aqua shirt, sipping my drink as I made up my mind. Just right, I thought, adding white sandals, small white earrings and coral lipstick, leaving my hair on my shoulders. I finished my drink and poured another. I didn't want to be early, that's for sure. Carrying on a conversation with Mr. Spencer, Tia, Dad and Meg would be a challenge and I needed my strength.

I washed the four plump tomatoes I'd brought in that afternoon. I was careful not to leave the fencing open this time. I wasn't going to let any more squirrels abscond with

Brian's garden bounty. I looked at the clock: 5:15 – time to leave. I gently placed the tomatoes in a grocery bag, finished my drink and popped a piece of gum in my mouth.

Since it was a Friday afternoon, the package store was busy. I made a beeline for the wine section. Since I was no expert, I would just spend more than I normally would. I was moving quickly, dodging other customers when I turned onto the wine aisle and nearly ran into a young woman moving as fast as I was.

"Scuse me," I said.

She let out a little squeal, clutching a bottle of wine.

"Jenna!"

She was wearing skinny white jeans with a bright print top that left her tummy bare and large hoop earrings.

"Tia!" I said, struggling not to meet her gaze.

"I'm taking a bottle of Cabernet to Dad's," she said, sounding like she'd been caught cheating on a test. "To go with the pot roast."

"Yeah, I had the same idea. But I'll choose something different."

"Good." She paused for a few seconds and then backed away. "Well, I'll see you there in a few minutes."

"Okay," I said, trying for a friendly, casual tone.

And she scurried off. I paid forty bucks for a bottle of Merlot and was on my way.

The reason Mr. Spencer was having this family dinner was obvious. He wanted to broker a peace treaty between me and his daughter. I would play along and do my best to make everyone happy. These were people I cared about.

When I pulled into the driveway, Tia's car was parked behind Dad's SUV, which was behind Mr. Spencer's car on the left side. So I pulled into the driveway on the right. I remembered when the Spencers closed in the carport to expand their living room and figured they might be watching me right now through the windows directly in front of my car. I summoned my courage, along with my bag of tomatoes and the bottle of wine, and forced myself to the front door.

"Jenna!" Mr. Spencer cried, pulling me into a warm embrace. "Come on in. Your Dad and Meg are here. And Tia just arrived."

I followed him through the living room to the kitchen, which was a mouthwatering hub of activity. I handed the wine to Dad who looked impressed after checking the label. Then I pulled out the tomatoes, which everyone went on and on about.

"Have you taken up gardening?" Mr. Spencer asked.

"I can't take any credit," I conceded. "My yard man is in charge of the garden. He just gives me fresh produce."

"Wow!" said Meg. "There's nothing like a homegrown tomato!"

Bowls and platters of food were whisked to the dining room table, which was decorated in an African motif – zebra striped plates encircled by a rim of deep red, and matching small red bowls. The tablecloth looked like a brightly colored African rug. As Meg gushed about the décor, I was breathing a sigh of relief that there was a wine glass at every place. We took our seats and Mr. Spencer poured the wine, except for Meg, of course, whose glass he filled with water.

Mr. Spencer took the seat at the head of the table opposite Tia on the other end. I sat across from Dad and Meg.

"So, Jenna," Mr. Spencer said, passing the platter of roast beef to Meg, "your dad tells me you're headed for New York!"

"That's right," I said, putting my napkin in my lap.

With prompting from Dad and Meg, Mr. Spencer asked me about the play I was being cast in next, the Brooklyn theater where Sam was hired, where we would be living, my experience in *Steel Magnolias* and what that theater was like. All this, as we gorged on Mr. Spencer's perfect roast and potatoes, Meg's spicy stuffed squash, fresh, home-cooked green beans that somebody made, thick slices of the best tomatoes in the world, buttery rolls Tia had brought and some pretty good wine, if I do say so myself. I was working on my third glass when I decided that was enough about me and asked Tia what she was up to.

"Well, I've got a modeling gig next week."

"Tell everyone what kind of photo shoot it is," Mr. Spencer said, grinning mischievously.

"It's for a toothpaste ad." And she flashed her perfect white teeth.

"And tell them about your last photo shoot," said Mr. Spencer, chuckling and shaking his head.

"I was a jeans model."

"From the rear," her dad added, laughing again.

I could feel Tia's indignation rising.

"How'd you get the jobs?" I asked.

"Through a modeling agency."

"You should check into that too, Jenna," Mr. Spencer said. "You've got the looks for modeling." And he turned again to Tia. "Maybe you could put her in touch with the right folks at the agency."

Tia screwed up her mouth for a moment and then pasted a tight smile on her face.

"I'm not really interested in modeling," I said, trying to rescue her. "That's a different skill set from acting."

She cleared her throat but said nothing and her dad steered the conversation to Meg and Dad's baby. They made self deprecating jokes about being middle-aged parents and rushing to have a baby before they had grandchildren.

Mr. Spencer pushed the button on the coffee pot and I refilled my wine glass as we adjourned to the living room, which was decorated in creams and tans with bright splashes of color and a wall of abstract jazz posters. As we took our seats, he opened the door of the hutch and pulled out a large, expensive leather photo album.

"I thought you all might be interested in looking at this," he said. "It's the result of months of research by my friend Ethel Robertson, who is a certified genealogist, along with the results of DNA testing we had done. Ethel traced some branches of our family back several centuries." He handed the album to Dad and Meg and gestured for me

and acts all holier than thou because she's an actress!"

Then she snatched my wine glass out of my hand.

"And…" she continued, nearly yelling now, "she accuses *me* of being an alcoholic! But look who's had – what is it – fourteen glasses of wine?"

I shouldn't have, but I couldn't help it – I reached for the glass to take it back and she splashed the wine in my face. My eyes stung and I squeezed them shut, causing my head to swim. I felt like I was falling. Someone handed me a paper towel and I blotted my eyes and face, aware of angry voices around me. God, I needed to get out of there! That's all I knew. I pushed past everyone and grabbed my purse, sprinting for the front door. Dad called my name as I stumbled toward the driveway but I kept going. I cranked the car and slammed it in Reverse to get the hell out of there, then hit the gas. But instead of backing out of the driveway, the car zoomed straight for the house! I tried to find the brake but it all happened too fast. I screamed as the car hurtled forward, crashing through the living room wall.

25.

When I came to, I was in a quiet place. My head throbbed and my chest felt like someone had taken a bat to me. There was a voice but it was muffled and I couldn't understand, drifting off again.

No idea how much later, I awoke from a deep sleep and realized I hurt all over. I couldn't bring myself to open my eyes because I knew it would make the pain worse. I lay there breathing and listening. Distant sounds of people moving about and talking. I realized someone was holding my hand.

"Jenna?"

A man's voice, a good voice. But opening my eyes was too hard so I said something, I think, and drifted back to sleep.

When I finally opened my eyes it was dark. A small lamp provided enough light for me to make out that I was in a hospital room, an I-V in my arm. Just breathing was painful, which was scary. I closed my eyes again.

"Jenna?"

It was the same voice from earlier. He was sitting by my bed but I was too weak to open my eyes. There were words, some his, some mine, I think. And then more sleep.

Bright sunlight against my eyelids. Way too much. I squeezed my eyes tight.

"Jenna? Can you hear me?"

My eyelids struggled open. Dad was standing at the foot of my bed. He looked as bad as I felt, his face drawn, his brows knotted.

"You suffered a concussion and you've got a couple of fractured ribs," he said, but he didn't come around to the side of the bed. "And a lot of bruises and scrapes. The doctor has you on some pretty strong pain medicine so you can breathe normally because it hurts to breathe when you have fractured ribs. Don't try to get out of bed without someone helping you."

I didn't know what to say and couldn't make my mouth work anyway.

"Do you understand?" he asked.

His voice was too loud so I closed my eyes again.

"I'll be back later to check on you."

And he was gone. But the bright light remained. If only the blinds were closed.

Then someone was holding my hand. It was a man's hand, I could tell, and I thought it was Dad. But when I opened my eyes I saw it was Brian. He had pulled a chair close to the bed on my left.

"Hi," he said softly.

It puzzled me that he was here and Dad was not. I sighed and my chest was racked with pain.

"Your dad's with Meg," he said. "She was injured in the crash. But not too badly. The baby's fine. She's in a room on the fifth floor."

"Crash?" I said, surprised how weak my voice sounded.

"The doctor says you might not remember the accident but that's normal."

It was normal to suffer amnesia? I was so confused and tired and woozy.

"Meg?"

"She's fine. Don't worry."

And then he jumped up, crossed the room and closed the blinds like he'd read my mind. As soon as the light dimmed I must've relaxed because I fell asleep again.

*

On the third day of my hospital stay Tia showed up. She swept into the room, flipped on the overhead lights, opened the blinds and proceeded to pace back and forth.

"So, my dad's insurance agent says they're talking with your insurance company about paying for the repairs to the house. Of course he's pretty upset about the whole thing. It's like a bomb went off in there. And it'll be that way for a long time before the front wall is rebuilt and the interior is redone and he can buy new furniture. Oh, and then there's his car, which has front end damage. But, as Dad says, no one was killed. So that's a good thing. Of course, it's like a huge embarrassment. For him and for me."

"Tia…"

"I mean, *everyone* knows about it."

"How does everyone…"

"It was, like, the lead story on every local TV station. No one told you?"

She pulled her phone out of her bag and swiped a couple of times and then handed it to me. The Channel 9 news anchor reported they had breaking news – a car had crashed into a home. They went to Alex who was standing on the street in front of Mr. Spencer's home. It was dark outside but the TV lights showed my car lodged about two thirds of the way inside a gaping hole in the front of the house. Pieces of wood and roofing dangled over the car and there was yellow crime scene tape behind him.

"Katie, what started as a dinner for family and friends ended in near tragedy this evening as a guest at Louis Spencer's home here on Faison Avenue crashed her car through his front living room wall. Mr. Spencer declined to talk with us but we're told the guest, Jenna Stevens, had been drinking and may have rammed the house accidentally in her attempt to leave the dinner party. We talked earlier with Officer Brian Mitchell who was first on the scene."

Alex paused and stared into the camera for a few seconds and then a piece of video was shown with Brian – my very own yard man cop – speaking into Alex's Channel 9 microphone.

"We ordered a blood alcohol test based on witness

statements that the subject had consumed alcohol during the dinner. And while we won't get the results back for a few days, we have reason to believe the driver may have been impaired at the time of the accident."

I handed the phone back to Tia. I didn't want to see any more.

"It was the lead story on every station," she said. "So, like, everybody and their brother knows you were drunk when you crashed your frigging car smack dab into my father's living room!" She shook her head and resumed pacing.

I was mortified. My former boyfriend covered the most humiliating event of my entire life while my yard man ordered a blood alcohol test on me as I was rushed unconscious to the E.R.

"When I saw Alex and his cameraman pull up in front of Dad's house, I locked myself in the bathroom," she said, stuffing her phone back in her bag. "No way I was gonna let him know it was my dad's house, although he probably figured it out. Bad enough he knew it was you on that stretcher. Of course, I don't think he saw you close enough to recognize you and you were covered in blood anyway, but by the time he went on the air at eleven, he was report-ing your name. So I guess he got it from the cop."

I squeezed the button on the tube that increased my pain medication. And in a moment I felt the drug hit my brain and closed my eyes. She was still babbling as I slipped quietly away.

Dad was angry too when he stopped by that evening.

He said Meg was at home and he was taking a few days off to take care of her. He explained she'd been cut in several places by flying shards of glass but, fortunately, she'd turned away just in time so the injuries were on her back and the backs of her upper arms. But he said she was very sore.

"The doctor says you can go home any time," he said, "but your recovery will take a month or two. And you have to do breathing exercises to keep your lungs healthy. He says it'll be painful. So I've arranged for a home health nurse to come by once a day to help you with that and anything else you need. Because I'll be busy with Meg."

"Dad, I..."

"What the hell is going on? You nearly killed yourself and the rest of us with that stunt the other night, including my wife and child. Good God!"

"I'm sorry, Dad, I..."

"I'm not interested in excuses or apologies. I'm totally out of patience. If you need counseling, get it! If you want to talk – to really talk – let me know. I'm sick of the evasiveness and I'm tired of you never looking in my eyes anymore. Like right now."

He took three steps toward the door and stopped.

"I'll be here in the morning to take you home."

No hug. No smile. No taking my hand. No reassurances. There was a box of tissues on my night stand but it hurt to reach that far so I just used the sheet to wipe my eyes and nose. I wished Sam were here. He would smile at me and give me a hug and talk with me. But I suddenly realized he had no clue I was even in the hospital. My phone was on the night stand by the tissues. I could call him. But as I reached slowly for the phone it occurred to me that if I had two fractured ribs I couldn't be in his play. Rehearsals were set to begin in a week and a half. All my agonizing over joining him in New York was a moot point because I wouldn't be going to New York. At least not right away. He would give someone else my part. I wondered if he would give someone else my part in his life as well.

26.

I was standing at the bottom, gazing up the stairs to where all my clothes and things were stored in the guest room on the second floor. But the steps were way too steep and there were so many of them that it might as well have been Mount Everest. So I lay down in the living room instead.

Dad had driven me home, as promised, and helped me up the front porch steps and through the door. Then he carried in several bags of groceries and put them away in the kitchen. He tidied up a bit and then dashed upstairs for a moment before returning to the living room where I was resting on the sofa.

"You've got food to eat and the house is in good shape. A physical therapist named..." and he reached in his pocket for a slip of paper, "...named Brianna Williams will be here tomorrow afternoon at two o'clock to help you with your breathing exercises. And, you've got my number."

He nodded and glanced around like he was avoiding looking at me and then cleared his throat.

"How's Meg?" I asked.

"Her wounds are healing."

I started to say 'I'm sorry' but he cleared his throat again.

"Lock the door after me," he said, walking out the front door.

My eyes closed of their own accord. As I drifted off to sleep, it occurred to me I should send flowers to Meg. And maybe Mr. Spencer too. Yes, I would send flowers and a note of apology. Tomorrow.

*

For Meg, I ordered a potted blue hydrangea, knowing she would enjoy planting it and watching it bloom every summer. And I sent a card telling her how sorry I was about the accident and hoped she felt better very soon. For Mr. Spencer, I ordered a fresh bouquet of sunflowers and had the florist attach a note telling him how deeply sorry I was about the damage to his house and car. When I completed my online orders, I felt better for a moment. Of course, it was a small gesture on my part, all things considered. I found my checkbook, which I rarely used, and made out a check for a thousand dollars to Mr. Spencer. I still had money from my mother, although I knew if I didn't get a job at some point, it would run out. But it helped ease my guilt a tiny bit. To say I'd ruined his goodwill dinner was putting it mildly.

A drink would make me feel better. I grunted as I rose

from my seat, holding my rib cage. But when I opened the cabinet where I kept the bourbon and mixer, I found a box of Special K, cereal bars, several cans of soup, crackers and some other groceries. But no liquor. I looked in the other cabinets and the refrigerator. But there was no alcohol of any kind. Not even a bottle of wine. Dad! He removed them when he stashed the groceries. Maybe he hid them somewhere? No. That's what was in the green Publix bag he was carrying when he left.

And I was stranded. My car was parked in a junkyard somewhere, totaled. Well, I could order groceries and have one of those home delivery services bring them to me. Including a bottle of wine. Or I could take Uber to the package store. But that was an overwhelming prospect right now. I retrieved my phone to search for a delivery service and found a text from Sam responding to the message I'd sent him before I left the hospital.

"No problem. Found a perfect actress to play Rachel. And she needed a fourth person for her apartment so I sublet a room. Feel better soon."

Which made me wonder when he'd cast her as the Goth girl – before I messaged him about my accident or after. I'd been so ambivalent about going to New York that it hadn't really crossed my mind that maybe he had mixed feelings too. I felt blindsided, deflated. I thought of my visionsight episode on closing night of *Magnolias* and wondered if his enthusiasm for my acting abilities might've cooled.

I sat down at the kitchen table, staring at his message,

and jumped when the phone rang in my hand. It was Brian. I almost didn't answer but then it crossed my mind that maybe I could ask him to bring me a bottle of something.

"Hello."

"Jenna, Brian. You at home?"

"Yes."

"Mind if I drop by to do a little gardening?"

"Of course not."

"I have a young friend I'd like to bring along, if that's okay."

"Sure."

"Great. We'll be there around seven. Can I pick up anything for you on my way?"

My mouth opened but closed again as I remembered – oh yeah, he's the police officer who charged me with DUI. What the hell was I thinking?

"I'm fine."

I searched online till I found a personal shopper who said, yes, she could buy a bottle of wine for me along with the rest of my order and she could deliver it tomorrow. Jesus! Tomorrow! Even though Dad had stocked my cabinets, I made up a list and asked her to get a bottle of Merlot and a bottle of Chardonnay.

I took a pain pill slightly ahead of schedule, figuring I'd need it when the physical therapist came. She arrived right on time and I was glad I'd taken my meds. She taught me how to do coughing exercises while holding a pillow against my ribs. It hurt like hell. She said I was supposed to do that every couple of hours so I wouldn't get a lung infection. By the time we were through, I was ready for another pain pill. She reminded me, just like the doctor did, that I shouldn't drink alcohol while I was on the medication since it was a narcotic.

"Got it," I said, ready for her to leave.

I was feeling woozy again like I might throw up so I lay down for an afternoon snooze.

The doorbell woke me. The light coming through the windows told me it was evening. I'd slept a long time. Sitting up was a struggle. Standing would be even harder, so I waited a moment as the doorbell chimed again. When I finally opened it, Brian was standing there, a teen-aged boy beside him. His young friend was black, about half a head shorter than Brian, with large, friendly eyes.

"You sure you should be up?" Brian asked, a worried look crossing his face.

Instead of answering, I returned to the couch, lying down carefully. My pain meds had worn off but the thought of getting a glass of water and my pill was too much.

"When was the last time you had a pain pill?" he asked.

I shook my head slightly.

"Raymond, can you go in the kitchen there and get a glass of water?" he said, pointing the way.

Raymond disappeared and reappeared in an instant as Brian found my pill bottle on the coffee table. I lifted my head just enough to swallow and then collapsed again.

"I'm not sure you should be home by yourself," he said,

squatting down in front of me.

"I'm fine."

"You don't look fine."

"Had my first physical therapy. That's all."

He didn't say anything for a long time so I slipped into dreamland again. When I opened my eyes, it was dark and quiet. A streetlight provided a sliver of light through the window. I found a note on my phone from Brian saying he locked the door on his way out but would return the key tomorrow.

*

When he arrived I was sitting at the kitchen table with a glass of orange juice. He rang the bell and let himself in and called out to me.

"In the kitchen," I said.

The aroma of coffee and bagels followed him as he sailed into the room carrying two cups of coffee and a brown bag. He toasted two bagels before joining me at the table, setting out butter and cream cheese along with milk and sweetener for my coffee.

"You need more than juice," he said.

As we ate, he told me about Raymond, who he'd met through Big Brothers Big Sisters.

"You're a big brother?"

"Yeah, I've got two boys right now, Raymond and Carlos."

"You're a regular good Samaritan," I said, giving him what must've appeared to be a weak smile.

"Far from it. But you – Amy told me all about how you

took the outcasts under your wing in elementary school and middle school. That's how you became friends with Tia. You befriended her when no one else would. Amy says she feels guilty to this day for not following your lead. And for not making friends with you. She says she and a lot of the other girls resented you because they thought you were trying to be a saint."

I sipped my coffee.

"I didn't become a big brother until after I was a cop and had my eyes opened. Your eyes didn't need opening. You instinctively recognized the need even when you were a little girl, which is pretty damn amazing."

It was sweet of him to say all this stuff but I was too tired to sit up any longer and pushed myself up from the table to return to my roost, leaving half a bagel on my plate. He followed me into the living room.

"I'm not trying to flatter you," he continued. "I just wanted to remind you that you're a good person with a warm heart, just in case you've forgotten."

I don't know why exactly, but I began to cry.

"And I've thought a lot about what you told me in the hospital," he said.

"What did I tell you?"

"Your gift."

I think my heart skipped a beat.

"What gift?" I asked.

"The visionsight," he said.

27.

"What are you talking about?" I tried my best to seem puzzled.

"Well, you told me how you saw the little girl's future – the little girl in your class – and how you saw your friend Tia's future and your dad's. And you described what happened in the hospital when your mom died."

I sat for a moment, thinking back to someone holding my hand and the warm voice I remembered hearing. God, it was Brian. But it was all very fuzzy.

"And you told me you inherited it from your mother. That it ruined your life, that you don't want to see people's futures if you can't do anything to stop tragedies from happening."

I withdrew my hand from his, feeling completely exposed. He studied me in a gentle sort of way. Good Samaritan, indeed. He'd found another needy person to help. And I didn't like it.

"You can chalk the crazy talk up to a concussion and lots of meds," I said. "Sounds like I was raving like a lunatic."

He shook his head.

"I don't think so," he said. "I've heard druggies ranting and raving before."

I shifted slowly, wincing as I put my feet on the coffee table.

"I know you didn't mean to share your secret. But I think it's good you finally told someone. It's too much of a burden to carry all by yourself.

I swallowed hard, trying to keep my emotions in check.

"Brian, really..."

"I'm honored you chose to tell me. Of course, maybe it was easier to tell someone outside your inner circle. Sometimes that's the way it is. And I want you to know I believe you."

His kindness was hard to take. Not sure why, but it was. I really didn't want his pity.

"It happens when you look in their eyes?" he asked softly.

"Brian, there's no such thing as – what did you call it – visionsight?"

"But you don't see everyone's future, just the people you care about?"

I closed my eyes.

"So you avoid looking at them," he continued.

"Brian..."

"And that's causing problems. I guess everyone thinks

you're pushing them away."

"It must've been a dream I told you about."

But he charged ahead.

"Have you tried making a difference, you know, changing an outcome for someone?"

"Stop."

I wanted him to leave.

"I was just wondering…" he said.

"Enough already!"

"…if you've tried to, you know, intercede to prevent…"

"Of course, I have!" I blurted, letting my emotions get the best of me and immediately wishing I could take it back. He was using his counselor technique on me, tricking me into talking.

"But have you looked again to see…"

I sat up suddenly, flinching from the exertion.

"God, you have no idea what it's like to see your own father's funeral as his widow holds their little boy's hand! You have no clue how painful it is! When I have one of these… these episodes, I feel like I've had the breath knocked out of me, like the blood's been drained from my body. I'm weak and shaky and can hardly stand. I should never have told you anything! What the hell were you doing in my hospital room anyway?"

I pulled myself up from the sofa and headed for the door, grunting in pain and wrapping my arms around myself, trying to keep my cracked ribs from moving. All this time I thought it would be a relief to tell someone my secret, but it wasn't. He didn't understand. He didn't know how agonizing it was. And, although he said he believed me, I wasn't at all convinced. He was obviously the kind of person who wanted to help people. In fact, he was probably humoring me – trying to help me work through what he viewed as a mental problem. Tears welled up again but I didn't want him to see me cry so I stood with my back to him to regain my composure.

"I'm very tired," I finally said. "And the physical therapist will be here soon."

"Okay. But before I go, I want to tell you something. I have a gift as well. Not quite as dramatic as yours, but sometimes I can see people's futures too. Like my buddy, Raymond. I saw his future the night I met him. That's when I arrested him for breaking into an elderly neighbor's house and pointing a gun at her. She caught him stealing the cash she kept hidden in her bedroom. He needed it for drugs. I didn't have to look in his eyes to see his future."

What I needed was another pain pill so I headed for the kitchen, Brian following right behind me.

"And when I look at you," he went on, "I see a very talented, smart, caring, beautiful person plummeting to earth without a parachute. Anyone who crashes into someone's house because she drank too much..."

"Get out!" I barked, grimacing in pain. I popped the Hydrocodone in my mouth, waving my hand at him.

"I'm trying to help," he said.

"By giving me a DUI and making me lose my license for a year? Thanks a lot!"

"You deserve to lose your license. You could've killed

someone, yourself included!"

"Out!"

I squeezed my eyes shut and doubled over.

"Jenna…"

"Go away."

"You're…"

"Who do you think you are?"

"I'm your friend. And I'm trying to help you."

"I don't need your help."

"Jenna…"

"I'll call the police," I said, looking for my phone.

By the time I found it, he was gone. I slumped on the couch, wishing my shopper would hurry up and get here with the wine. Why had I told Brian all those things? And how dare he talk to me like that? He had no concept what it was like. None. He couldn't even begin to imagine what I'd been through. I had been right to keep it a secret. No one would understand. They would all think I was crazy. My instincts had been correct all along. The best plan was to keep my distance from people. Simple as that. And I thought of Sam, the guy who sort of, but not quite, loved me. Who wanted to cast me in his plays. The guy who might be the key to my future in a place where I didn't have to suffer through those nightmarish visions.

I curled up in a fetal position and the next thing I knew the physical therapist was ringing the doorbell. I tried to beg off, telling her I was very sore but she insisted I do my coughing exercises. She nagged me and reminded me I was supposed to be doing the exercises on my own as well.

"You could develop pneumonia if you don't keep your lungs healthy," she said.

"Okay, okay!"

"And make sure you don't drink any alcohol," she said. "I'm sure the doctor told you that mixing alcohol with your meds could be lethal."

"I know!"

And she slapped a blood pressure cuff on my arm before I could object and told me my blood pressure was too high. But that didn't stop her from forcing me to do the damn exercises. By the time we finished I could hardly move and I was so pissed off at everyone in my life – myself included – that I wanted to scream. But I knew it would be agonizing for my ribs so I just gritted my teeth and held my head in my hands.

Just as she was packing up to leave, the doorbell rang again and my shopper was bringing in the groceries I'd ordered. Brianna showed herself out as I led the shopper to the kitchen. By law, she had to card me for the wine.

I was finally alone again with a bottle of red and a bottle of white. And then my phone rang in my pocket where I'd stuffed it after threatening to call the cops on Brian. I looked at the screen and debated whether to answer when I saw it was Mrs. Robertson. I finally relented, hoping for information about my dad.

"Jenna, you won't believe what I've discovered!

"Uh..."

"It's a first for me, that's for sure."

"I..."

"I'm not far from your house. Mind if I stop by? I'd really like to tell you in person."

I wanted badly to say no but she sounded so excited that I gave in. I was going to open the white wine and offer her – and myself – a glass but I couldn't find a corkscrew. Just as the doorbell rang I realized Dad had been more thorough than I realized when he stole my Jim Beam.

"Lovely home," Mrs. Robertson said, filling the living room with her smile.

"I don't have much in the way of drinks but would you like a cup of tea?"

"Ice water would be perfect," she said, following me into the kitchen and taking a seat at the table like she owned the place. "I find I have more energy if I avoid caffeine and sugar. You should try it!"

I smiled and fixed us both a glass of ice water, setting them on the table along with a couple of napkins.

"Okay," she said. "Are you ready?"

I nodded and shrugged my shoulders at the same time. We were sitting directly across from each other and she leaned in like she was about to whisper a huge secret that she didn't want anyone else to hear.

"You're descended from a woman who was burned at the stake as a witch."

Mrs. Robertson laughed. I did not. Of course, she had no clue that it confirmed my worst fears about my gift, or curse, or whatever you want to call it.

"She's the reason your ancestors left Ireland to come to America. They had to salvage their reputation somehow, so they packed up and moved to the new world."

She took a sip of water, then pulled her laptop from her bag and opened it on the table in front of her. She referred to her notes as she continued.

"Sarah Campbell was your twelfth great grandmother. She was born Sarah Brown and married a man named Donald Campbell in 1701. But twelve years later she was tried for witchcraft and sentenced to death. Some of the villagers said she claimed to see their future. And when she predicted a neighbor would have a stillborn child and it came true, her own family turned against her, believing she put a hex on the baby."

She shook her head as she continued talking, not noticing my distress.

"Even though Sarah had two children of her own, she was burned at the stake." She shook her head. "Can you imagine?"

I swallowed hard and took a sip of water, not knowing what to say because the fact of the matter was – I *could* imagine.

"Donald took the children and left County Tipperary, making the long ocean voyage to America. They became indentured servants in Virginia, all three of them: Donald; his eleven-year-old son, Seamus; and his nine year old daughter Brigid."

She shook her head again.

"I've never uncovered anything like this. And I have to tell you my mouth fell open as I read the account in a letter from Brigid to her daughter many years later. Obviously, the experience of losing her mother like that really hit Brigid hard. She warned her own daughter to keep to herself and not let other people know her business. She also told her if she ever thought she was having a premonition, not to tell anyone about it. Understandable under the circumstances, don't you think?"

While I knew no one would be burned at the stake anymore, I was petrified that if people thought I was psychotic... well, only bad things could come from that. And I wondered if Brian would keep my secret. He was close to his sister. What if he told her? And then what if she told someone else? What if Brian went to Dad and Tia and told them? Was it possible they might try to have me committed?

"But Brigid's daughter, Eileen, apparently ignored her mother," Mrs. Robertson continued, referring to her notes again. "She became a psychic after Brigid died and actually earned money telling customers' futures by gazing into a crystal ball. Isn't that fascinating?"

She grinned from ear to ear, reveling in her successful sleuthing. I forced myself to smile in reply even though there was no joy in my heart. Maybe she finally noticed my discomfort because she shifted gears then.

"I should've asked how you're doing," she said. "I heard about your accident. Are you in a lot of pain?"

"Not too bad," I lied.

"Well, I better go. You look like you need some rest."

She closed her laptop, slipped it back in her bag, took her glass to the sink and strode through the living room as I followed her to the front door.

"You want me to keep poking around?" she asked as she opened the door.

"Sure, that would be great," I said, although, at the moment, I was uncertain whether I really wanted to know any more or not.

"All righty, then. I'll be in touch again soon. Feel better!"

*

I was in agony. Excruciating pain. I writhed as the flames scorched my flesh. I was tied to a tall pole, ropes wrapped tightly around me. My clothes were in flames and the ropes were burning as well. An angry, self-righteous mob watched with cruel satisfaction as the fire grew hotter. Not an ounce of pity in those hateful eyes. I opened my mouth and a terrifying scream rose from the depths of my soul and I bolted upright, with tears streaming down my face. I grabbed my rib cage and looked around the room.

I'd fallen asleep with my laptop beside me. I never should've looked at all those awful drawings and paintings posted online of witch burnings.

*

Because I stayed up half the night, spooked about having another nightmare, I was very late getting up the next day and barely had enough time to get to my doctor's appointment to check my ribs. I took a Lyft car, preferring not to ask anyone for a ride.

Dr. Abrams told me I was doing all right but to continue my coughing exercises for another week and to be patient.

On my way out, I felt someone staring at me as I walked through the waiting room, and glanced in her direction. It was Randall Hayes' wife, Wendy. Her blonde hair was pulled into a pony tail and she had on minimal makeup and was wearing black slacks and a grey jacket – nothing like the plunging cocktail dress she had on the last time I saw her. I kept walking, but she called my name and followed me to the door. When I stalked out of the cast party that night after telling her I wasn't the one Randall was cheating with, I hoped I'd never see either of them again. But no such luck.

"I've got a car waiting for me," I said.

I pushed the door open and stepped outside in the heat and humidity. But she was right behind me.

"I just need a minute," she said.

Although it crossed my mind she might pull the gun on me that she'd bragged about, I reluctantly turned to face her.

"I wanted to thank you," she said, totally taking me by surprise. "Even though it was a humiliating scene at the party, you helped me face the truth. I left Randall and I'm filing for divorce."

I opened my mouth but didn't know what to say.

"I'm taking drama classes and auditioning for a role at a little theater way out in the suburbs. I don't know why I let him treat me that way, the rat. A repeat offender, as you put it."

"Wow," is all I could think of.

"So..."

"Well, I wish you the best. I really do," I said.

She nodded and I nodded and then I walked to the waiting car as she went back inside.

The driver drove like a maniac – too fast, too slow, turning at the wrong places. My body tried to compensate, my foot pressing the floor, instinctively attempting to apply the brakes, my hand squeezing the arm rest, trying to steer the car. Finally, we reached my grocery store and I went in to get a couple of things, including a corkscrew, before heading home.

I opened the Chardonnay and poured myself a glass and collapsed on the sofa, checking emails and messages. Three from Brian, one from Dad, one from Meg and one from Sam.

Surprisingly, Sam answered on the second ring.

"How the hell are ya?" he asked.

"I've been better but I've been worse," I said, trying for a light tone.

He laughed.

"Are you able to move around?" he asked.

"Oh yeah. I just have to take it kind of easy. How are you?"

"Love it up here. Course, I knew I would."

I think I was hoping he'd talk about missing me or say something about looking forward to my joining him or something, but he didn't. Maybe he was waiting for me to say something about missing him, but I wasn't sure I did. I was sort of hoping to feel a stirring of emotions but it didn't happen. Neither of us could think of much to say.

"Well, my physical therapist just pulled up in the driveway," I lied. "Good luck with everything."

I took a big swig of wine. And then several more before laying my head down.

And then I was being burned alive. Only this time I was somehow able to pull the ropes from my body and leap over the flames and run through the darkness to a car parked beneath a tree. I opened the driver's door, climbed inside, cranked the engine and pressed the gas, tires squealing as I raced down a country road with trees close on both sides. But I panicked when I realized there was no steering wheel. There was a crystal ball on the dash instead. I reached for it and pulled it close against my stomach as I leaned left and right, trying to keep the car from running off the road and into the trees. The car careened along the winding road until finally, I put both feet on the brake and the car came to a screeching halt. I was bathed in sweat. As I opened the door, the crystal ball slipped from my hands and shattered on the pavement.

My ribs were killing me when I woke up and realized today was my first appearance in DUI Court.

29.

My attorney's name was Paul Dixon – pudgy, middle-aged, grey-suited – recommended by a friend of a friend. He gave me an irritated glare when I arrived ten minutes late in front of the courthouse. But I think he approved of my appearance. I had chosen black slacks, a pale green, three-quarter sleeve top and low heels. My hair was on my shoulders and I was only wearing lip gloss and some Erase under my tired eyes.

I would plead not guilty and then he would get to work trying to have the DUI charge thrown out. Although he'd told me the arraignment was just a formality, I was on edge, which wasn't doing my ribs any good.

He led the way to a fourth floor courtroom where we took a seat and waited as a bailiff called each case. The judge, her staff and the guards looked like they were bored stiff while those of us in the gallery were, by and large, a bunch of nervous Nellies.

As we waited for my case to be called, I was alarmed to see Brian enter the courtroom on my right. It was unnerving how official he looked in his police uniform. I tried not to think back to the night of the accident, what he must've seen when he arrived, how I must've looked, how he would've interviewed everyone and then spoken on camera with the TV reporters. I took a slow, deep breath, trying to calm myself.

"Why is he here?" I whispered to Mr. Dixon, pointing at Brian.

"Is he the arresting officer?" he whispered back.

"Yes."

"I don't know. They don't usually come for arraignment."

And finally, the judge called my name and Mr. Dixon and I both walked to the front. A bailiff read the charges and the judge asked if I understood.

"Yes."

"Can't hear you," the judge said.

"Yes," I said, louder this time.

"How do you plead?"

"Not guilty," I replied, my voice quivering.

"Do you have an attorney?"

"Yes," I replied, looking at Mr. Dixon.

"Paul Dixon, your honor," he said, nodding at her.

She made a note and, without looking up, announced that my preliminary hearing would be held in four weeks. Then Mr. Dixon led me into the crowded hallway.

"I'll call you," he said, and headed back into the courtroom where he was representing another client.

I closed my eyes and heaved a sigh, not of relief, but of disgust. I didn't like being here in this environment with all kinds of law-breakers and miscreants. It made me feel cheap. I headed for the elevators but I didn't make a clean escape. Brian walked up as the elevator doors opened. It was already crowded and there was just enough room for the two of us. He nodded but didn't speak. We stood shoulder to shoulder for the ride to the first floor. When we piled off the elevator into the marble-floored lobby he followed me out the front door.

"Jenna," he said softly.

"Were you trying to intimidate me?" I asked, hurrying down the granite steps.

"No, I just..."

"Then why did you show up dressed in your uniform, standing there so you'd be sure I saw you?" I raised my voice as I headed for the street.

"Well..."

"You were trying to bully me into pleading guilty, weren't you?"

I don't know why but my voice cracked. I continued toward the street, looking for the Uber car I'd requested.

"Jenna," he said, stepping in front of me on the sidewalk.

But I went around him, groaning in exasperation, as I looked up and down the street for my car.

"Where the hell is he?" I snapped.

"Who?"

"My Uber ride."

"I can drive you."

"No, thanks!"

He shook his head as I continued scanning the street.

"You wanna know why I came today? Well, just turn around for a second and I'll tell you."

I didn't want to turn around. I wanted to get the hell out of there. But he stepped in front of me, very close to the curb, and looked down into my face. I studied the eagle wings on his police badge and swallowed hard.

"I came today because I care very much about you," he said, his voice soft and low.

I clamped my eyes shut as he put his hands on my shoulders, overwhelmed by conflicting emotions. I realized I'd been trying to tamp down the growing affection I felt, trying not to like him too much. Which was, no doubt, the reason I'd been so angry. But it wasn't really him I'd been mad at – it was my screwed up life. And now he knew my secret. Why had I blabbed at the hospital? Even if I was high on pain meds, why had I confided in *him*?

A horn honked close by and I jumped. It was my ride. I pulled away from him and headed into the street.

"Jenna, I just came off duty. Let me drive you."

I opened the back door.

"Please," he said, putting his hand on my arm. "Please."

His hand was so warm and gentle on my arm, that I hesitated. And when I did, he tossed a couple of bills to the driver, then closed the door and put his hand on my back.

"This way," he said.

We walked to the parking deck and got in his truck. I winced as I climbed into the front seat and knew I needed another pain pill. We drove in silence until we reached a tree-lined street on the edge of Decatur.

"I thought you were taking me home," I said.

"Well, I've got homemade zucchini soup in my crock pot. I think you could use a bowl of soup."

We pulled into the driveway of what would've been described in a real estate listing as a charming bungalow. It was a small, grey brick home surrounded by two huge magnolias, bushes and flowers, with a screened porch on the front. He helped me out of the truck and led the way.

We entered through the porch into a sunny living room with hardwood floors, a tan couch and a couple of overstuffed chairs. A large potted ficus tree stood in the corner and there was a big screen TV. We followed the aroma of homemade soup to an old-fashioned kitchen – knotty pine cabinets, red Formica and chrome table and chairs. Pots and pans hung above the stove.

"Make yourself at home," he said. "I'll change into my civvies and be right back."

I needed to sit down but more than that, I needed a pain pill. So I fixed myself a glass of water from the tap, swallowed the capsule, and gazed out the window above the sink to the back yard. Half the yard was a lush garden. I spotted tomatoes and green beans and what looked like cucumbers. Of course, maybe they were zucchinis, since he was cooking zucchini soup. A thick carpet of grass covered the other half of the yard, with pretty violet asters along the fence. Several cushioned lawn chairs sat on a patio. They looked so inviting that I unlocked the sliding glass door and wandered out back to sit down. The sun felt good on my face so I closed my eyes and leaned my head back on the cushion, folding my arms across my rib cage.

Then I was driving a shiny black car, using a crystal ball because there was no steering wheel and no pedals. I was escaping the fire and had burn marks where ropes had tied me to the stake. I was on that winding road again with tree branches closing in above me, in a full-blown panic.

"Jenna, Jenna," a voice called.

I opened my eyes, feeling disoriented and lost. Brian was on his knees beside me, holding my shoulder.

"It's all right. You were dreaming," he said.

I took a deep breath, feeling the need for more oxygen.

"I should've taken you home," he said. "You must be exhausted."

"I'm fine."

I saw him out of the corner of my eye studying me for a moment.

"How about some soup?"

And we returned to the kitchen where he had set the table with bowls, plates, silverware and napkins, along with a serving plate of sliced tomatoes, pickles and wheat crackers.

"How long did I sleep?" I asked, taking my seat.

"About half an hour," he said, ladling steaming soup into the bowls. I could see bits of zucchini, tomato, onion, celery and green pepper.

He returned the crock pot to the kitchen counter, fixed two glasses of ice water and sat down on my left, leaving me a clear view of the back yard through the sliding glass door.

"What were you dreaming?" he asked, forking a slice of tomato onto my plate.

"I was driving a car."

"Hm."

"Except it didn't have a steering wheel, a gas pedal or a brake pedal."

"No wonder you cried out."

"I screamed?"

"It sounded more like moaning," he said. "Cracker?"

I shook my head and put a spoonful of the soup in my mouth. It transported me back momentarily to when I was a little girl when Dad used to say that Grandma's soup was so good, it warmed his cockles. This was that kind of soup.

"What happened?" he asked.

I considered whether to tell him but figured it couldn't hurt at this point.

"Well, I was scared to death, trying to drive the car with a crystal ball."

"A crystal ball?"

"Yeah, the kind of crystal ball a psychic might use."

He was looking at me, waiting for more.

"The soup is incredible," I said.

"Anything else?" he asked.

"Well, I was escaping being burned at the stake as a witch."

He made a small guttural sound, set his spoon down and reached over to touch my arm.

"I'm a good driver, you know," I said. "This is the second time I've dreamed about driving a car with no steering wheel. And I was better at it this time, better at keeping the car on the road. It's like I could send a message to the car through the crystal ball."

And I chuckled.

"It was like the car became an extension of my body, just like in real life," I continued. "That's how I feel when I'm driving – almost like the car knows what I want it to do before I consciously think about it. Except, of course, for that night at Mr. Spencer's house."

He nodded but, unlike some people I knew, refrained from making any smartass comments.

We made small talk as we ate. He didn't press me further about my dream, which was good. When we'd had our fill, he stored the rest of the soup in the fridge but left the dishes for later. When I rose from the table he crossed the room to stand in front of me.

"You're not looking at me anymore," he said. "You haven't looked at me at all today. And I'm not entirely sure you looked at me yesterday, although I didn't realize it at the time."

I gritted my teeth, studying the button on his black polo shirt, which, I confess, looked very good on him.

"Does that mean…" he said, and stopped.

"That means I'm afraid."

"You're not alone anymore," he whispered. "Now close

your eyes."

"Why?"

"Just close your eyes for a minute."

When I did, he pulled me into a gentle embrace and put his mouth on mine, kissing me tenderly. And I found myself returning his kiss and wanting more.

"I love you, Jenna."

30.

I must've flinched as we made the short drive home. I desperately needed to lie down. Brian reached over to hold my hand as we drove.

"Have you been to the doctor lately?" he asked.

"Yeah. He says I'm fine. It'll just take time."

I could feel him looking at me.

"Remember the guy who played my husband in *Rose and Lily*?"

"Yeah?"

"I ran into his wife as I was leaving the doctor's office. Or maybe I should say ex-wife."

"Oh?"

"She left him."

"That surprises you?"

"Very much."

"Why?"

"Well, I had a vision with Randall during rehearsals and

I saw him cheating on his wife with the actresses he worked with."

"But I thought you only…"

"Yeah, but Sam had told me to really get into character and I was trying hard to feel the emotion of the moment when Randall was supposed to kiss me in the moonlight. And, well, I guess I got so totally into character that when I looked into his eyes, I saw his future."

"Damn!"

And then I told him about the unpleasant scene at the cast party when I spilled the beans about Randall's infidelities after Wendy accused me of having an affair with him.

He pulled the truck into the driveway and turned off the engine. But we just sat there.

"That's very interesting," he finally said.

"Yeah, I was thinking the same thing. Because it finally dawned on me that if Wendy left Randall, then what I saw in his eyes won't happen. At least, she won't be the wife he comes home to and makes excuses to."

"So…"

"Something changed. What I saw won't play out the way I saw it."

He jumped out of the truck and walked around to my side, opening the door to help me out. Then he wrapped his arms around me and held me carefully.

"You did it," he said.

When he stepped back, I was feeling reassured and hopeful for the first time in forever. And, of course, I'd been so used to looking at him since that day I found him on my doorstep, that I looked straight into his smiling brown eyes. For an instant, I could see the love in his heart, but then my knees buckled as I was thrown headlong into a harrowing dream-like sequence.

It was dark and rainy and he was running and running, panting hard as he raced between two buildings. As he ran under a streetlight, I could see a gun in his hand. There was the crackling of a walkie-talkie as he charged ahead. And then there was a loud popping noise – gunfire – and he hit the ground as voices on the walkie-talkie continued hissing into the night. Footsteps faded into the distance as though someone were running away on wet pavement. Then it was dark and quiet and I came to, dizzy and weak, with Brian holding me in his arms, my cheeks wet with tears.

"Jenna, are you all right?"

His voice seemed so far away.

"Jenna?"

But I couldn't speak. The horror of what I'd seen was too much to bear.

He walked me inside and helped me lie down in my usual spot, handing me a tissue. He sat beside me, but didn't say anything. He waited patiently for me to speak. But I couldn't bring myself to talk about it. It was like my heart had taken a sucker punch. I lay there until the tears finally stopped.

"Tell me what you saw," he said.

"You... you were chasing someone with your gun

drawn. And then there was gunfire and you were shot and I… I saw you die."

My voice cracked and tears welled up again. He put another tissue in my hand and I blotted my eyes.

"It's all right," he said. "It's all right."

"No, it's not all right."

He faced the window, watching me out of the corner of his eye.

"Listen, you just told me how you changed what happened with that actor and his wife."

I opened my eyes and looked at the side of his handsome face. His jaw was set like he was ready to go into battle. He nodded his head and put his hand on my arm, giving it a tiny squeeze, still looking across the room. Was it really possible that warning him would protect him?

"Any idea when that scene takes place?" he asked.

"No."

"Did you see anyone besides me?"

"I just heard footsteps. And voices on a walkie-talkie. And gunfire."

He nodded thoughtfully and I saw his Adam's apple bob as he swallowed. I wondered if he was as frightened as I was.

"I think you need to rest and I need to run a couple of errands," he said, and he leaned down and held me close, kissing my forehead. "I'll come back this evening. Don't worry, okay? Everything will be all right."

"You think?"

"Hell, yeah."

He kissed me again and locked the door on his way out, taking a key with him. I really needed to drift off to sweet, restful sleep. But I couldn't stop the vision from playing over and over in my head. And I dreaded being burned at the stake again and the panic that overwhelmed me as I used a ridiculous crystal ball to drive a car.

"Shit!" I yelled at the ceiling.

I forced myself up, triggering a spasm of pain in my ribs. Another pill, that's what I needed. I hobbled to the kitchen, trying to remember when I'd taken the last one. I poured myself a glass of wine instead and headed out the back door. I wandered around the garden looking at the fruits of Brian's labor. I wasn't sure when I'd fallen in love with him. I didn't even realize I had until today. And now that we had found each other it was torture to think I would lose him.

"It's not fair," I cried.

I was so tired but I was terrified of the dream. I wished Mrs. Robertson had never told me about my poor twelfth great grandmother who was burned at the stake. I thought about her daughter, the one who was concerned for her own daughter, afraid she might be accused of sorcery. So much so, that she told her not to let anyone know she had any kind of psychic abilities. But it was amazing that the daughter – what was her name, Ellen, Ila, Eileen, yes, Eileen – it was amazing Eileen ignored her mother and made a living from her talent. With a crystal ball!

And that's when it hit me. If she made money telling people's fortunes, she must've been able to control her visions so she could see people's futures when she *wanted* to. And it dawned on me that I had accidentally done that. I'd seen Randall's future, hadn't I? And Judy's. Even though I didn't like them one bit. I suddenly wanted to know more about Eileen and fired off an email to Mrs. Robertson.

I set my empty wine glass in the sink and was struck by how it sparkled in the sunlight. I thought again of the crystal ball in my dreams. Ever since Mrs. Robertson told me about Eileen, I'd been dreaming of using a crystal ball to drive my getaway car. I fixed myself a cup of coffee and brought my laptop to the kitchen table where I did a little research about crystal balls. As I sipped my coffee I concluded they were used mainly as a stage prop to convince customers or an audience that magic was being performed. But it appeared they were also used as a means of focusing the mind, something to stare into so you weren't distracted. And I thought any number of things could be used to help you focus the mind – a pattern on a computer screen or maybe a wine glass.

I returned to the sink and picked up the empty glass, holding it up to the light. Was it possible to drive my vision-sight episodes like I drove a car? I remembered my words about the experience of driving, that the car seemed to be an extension of my body, that my hands and feet responded without conscious thought, almost by instinct.

My mind was racing – could I look into someone's eyes and search for something, in particular? Like exactly what would kill my father. Or who would shoot Brian. I swallowed hard as I tried to avoid visualizing that horrific scene. But I made up my mind that I had to try. I had no clue how I'd go about it, but it could be that my dream was a message from my subconscious that if I could drive a car with no steering wheel, I might be able to drive my visions.

31.

"So how does this work?" he asked.

I shrugged.

We were sitting next to each other on the couch. I'd explained to Brian what I wanted to do when he arrived with quesadillas for supper.

"Maybe we should eat first," he said.

But the thought of intentionally triggering a vision was making my heart race.

"Let's just get it over with," I said.

"Okay. You stay where you are."

I got his drift. That way I would already be seated and wouldn't fall. So I shifted around, folding my legs underneath me. He took my hands in his and kissed each one.

"Wait," he said, leaning closer, his eyes focused on my mouth. He closed his eyes and kissed me – a long, sweet kiss – as he held my face in his hands.

Then he moved away slightly. I took a deep breath and

tried to relax.

"Brian," I said softly.

And when he looked at me I gazed straight into his eyes, concentrating with all my might on seeing everything I could possibly see.

Didn't matter that I did it on purpose. I was rocked by the vision, this time a young man – he looked familiar – lying on the floor in front of a counter in a store, blood on his chest and the tiles, Brian stooped beside him, holding his hand. The boy said something and then went limp, his eyes staring, sightless, at the ceiling. An older man behind the counter, pointing and shouting something. Brian's voice, the crackle of the walkie-talkie. Then running out the door into the night, running and panting into the dangerous darkness. Then a glimpse of someone racing ahead of him under a streetlight – a tall, slender man with a gun in his hand. No, no, no! The popping of gunfire and everything went black. I gasped and covered my face with my hands as I came to. My chest hurt but I wasn't sure if it was my cracked ribs or my heart breaking.

"Shh, it's all right. I'm here."

He pulled me onto his lap, holding me until I calmed down and my pulse rate slowed.

"Oh, Brian. Your young friend – I can't remember his name – he was killed."

"Raymond?"

"Yes, the boy you brought over here, he was shot dead in a store. I think it was a theft... what do you call it?"

"Armed robbery?"

"Yes. The man behind the counter pointed to where the guy with the gun went and you took off after him."

He sat quietly for a moment, obviously as shaken as I was.

"Anything else? Did anyone say anything?"

"Raymond said something to you but I couldn't hear."

"Hm."

"And the man behind the counter shouted something."

He sighed heavily, lost in thought. I tried to remember more but I never heard what was being said.

"Did you see what the gunman looked like?" he asked.

"No. He was just a dark shadow in the dim light of the streetlamp. Except he was tall and thin."

"Tall and thin."

"Yeah."

"What about the man behind the counter? What did he look like?

"He was Asian, I think."

We sat for a moment, both lost in thought. He held me close, rubbing my back and kissing my cheek.

"You need some food," he said. "And so do I."

We took our quesadillas out on the patio so we could look at the garden and not each other, sitting side by side at the table. Not much conversation, though, as we ate.

"Thank you, Jenna. I know that was hard. But what you saw could help me save Raymond's life."

"And yours."

"Yeah, that too. I don't know how you did it, but you were able to expand your vision."

"It would help a lot more if we knew who that guy was."

"Well, I'm gonna talk with Raymond."

"If only I could hear what they were saying. Maybe I should try again."

"I don't want to put you through…"

"Brian, we're talking about your life and Raymond's life. If I can focus on hearing the words."

Now that I had such a strong motivation, I realized I wasn't as fearful of the visions as I was before.

"I don't know."

"I'll survive."

I could feel him looking at me as he mulled it over and I decided now was as good a time as any, and I returned his gaze before he could look away, concentrating with all my might on hearing.

My senses were overwhelmed by noise as though the volume was too high on the TV. A call came in over his police radio – armed robbery in progress. He swung his patrol car around in a squealing U-turn and roared down the street with his siren blaring and blue lights flashing. The noise was unbearable. Then screeching to a stop in front of a small store, running inside, gun drawn, to find Raymond lying in a pool of blood on the floor. Brian squatting next to him, leaning close. Raymond whispering a name, Mike? A frantic Asian man behind the counter shouting: "He point gun at me!" The man gesturing toward the street. Brian rushing out into the darkness, running, running into a trap. I heard the gunfire and saw Brian fall.

In the distance I could see the tall, thin man with the gun under a streetlight. And I gulped hard as I regained consciousness, Brian's hand on my arm. Then I leaned away from him and threw up.

He helped me inside to the kitchen sink where I rinsed my mouth, then practically carried me to the living room so I could lie down. If I'd been drained before, I was totally spent now. Even if it ended in a nightmare, I had to sleep. But before I did, I told him what I'd heard. He kissed me and said he'd be back in the morning.

"You're not going to work, are you?"

I was afraid what I'd seen would happen very soon since I hadn't seen anything else – no other life events. And I could feel myself breaking out in a cold sweat.

"No, I've got a couple of days off. Don't worry."

*

The sleep of the dead. I don't like that expression but it describes the peaceful slumber I experienced. Finally, no nightmare. I wasn't burned at the stake and I didn't have to use a crystal ball to make my escape. But when I awoke the next morning, my ribs were throbbing. So I started my day with a pain pill and coughing exercises before making my way slowly up the stairs to take a shower.

After I dried off and was putting my lotion on, the light over the mirror popped and went dark. I thought about waiting and asking Brian to replace the bulb when he came over but he already did so much and I didn't want to feel like a helpless female. So I slipped on my short kimono and found a bulb in the drawer, then used the toilet as a step stool to climb onto the counter. I unscrewed the globe on the light fixture but lost my grip and it bounced off the counter and crashed to the floor, shattering in a spray of glass.

"Dammit."

And then I heard footsteps bounding up the stairs and Brian's voice calling my name. He burst into the bathroom, reeking of bacon, taking in the scene with a quick glance.

"Don't move," he snapped. "I don't want you to cut your feet on the glass."

"The light burned out."

"Why didn't you ask me…"

"I didn't know you were here."

"Would you please make sure that pitiful little excuse for a robe doesn't come open?"

He crossed the room and motioned for me to lean down so he could carry me.

"Because if it comes open," he said, "I can't guarantee I'll continue to act like a gentleman."

He carried me from the bathroom, stepping carefully over the shards of glass. When we got to the door, he slipped off his shoes and continued across the carpet, setting me gently on the bed.

"You're too kind," I said, adjusting my robe.

"No, I'm not. I'll tell you what I am. Right now, I'm more turned on than I've ever been in my entire life. And if you didn't have those cracked ribs and I didn't have bacon in the frying pan and biscuits in the oven, I might rip that sexy robe off and…"

Which made me smile.

"Do me a favor," he called, hurrying from the room. "Put on some loose, frumpy clothes and come down for breakfast." And he jogged down the stairs.

Breakfast was crisp bacon, scrambled eggs, biscuits and coffee.

"Thanks for getting dressed," he said, nodding at my capris and tee shirt as we sat down at the kitchen table.

There was something about sitting next to him with steam rising from our coffee cups and bowls of real food in front of us that made me feel loved. Here was a man who would cook a homemade breakfast for me without any prompting. A man who grew vegetables in a garden that he planted himself. A man who nurtured others. A man willing to risk loving me first despite all the baggage I brought with me, which was plenty.

Instead of doctoring my coffee, I placed my hand on his arm.

"I need to tell you something," I said.

I could feel his muscle flex beneath my fingers.

"Because I haven't actually said it yet," I whispered.

He let out his breath.

"I'm so in love with you," I said.

"You're bound and determined to ruin our breakfast," he said, leaning over to kiss me.

"I want you," I whispered.

"You're too...

"We can go slowly."

I led the way upstairs where we removed each other's

clothes and he laid me carefully on the bed and kissed and caressed my body. I kept my eyes closed as we made the most blissful, sweet love to each other, the likes of which I'd never experienced. It was so much more than enjoying a steak. Being with Brian was like the joining of two spirits. I held him close afterwards, feeling his heart pounding against my chest. Or was it my heart pounding against his?

"Jenna, Jenna, Jenna," he whispered.

32.

We finally had breakfast – reheated biscuits and bacon – and he scrambled up a fresh batch of eggs and fixed another pot of coffee. We were both famished.

"I went over to see Raymond last night," he said, digging into the eggs.

"How'd it go?"

"Well, we walked over to the elementary school and shot some baskets. Some other kids were there too. I had my eyes peeled for a tall, skinny kid. Then, as we were walking back to his apartment these two guys were headed straight for us. Both of them were tall and thin. And one of them calls out to Raymond 'you coming with us to the show?' And Raymond says 'yeah, I'll be over in a few.' He didn't introduce me or anything. So when we were out of earshot I asked him if they were friends from school. And he says 'yeah, Stefon and Ike.' So I asked him if they're good guys to hang out with and he says 'yeah.' I said 'you sure?'

And he says 'yeah.' I asked him how long he'd known them and he said since ninth grade, that they live in the next apartment complex over. So I asked him what their last names were and he told me Stefon Brown and Ike Redding. Made up names for sure. And when we got to his place I talked with him about how important it was for him to graduate and go to college. Talked about taking him on some college visits this fall. But something's changed. Or maybe I'm just on high alert now."

He sipped his coffee.

"So he went up to his room to get ready and I talked with his mom for a few minutes. And she told me he's been hanging out with some new guys and she's concerned. Said he won't tell her anything about them but he's been staying out late again."

"Jeez."

"When he came downstairs he was surprised I was still there. I walked out with him and told him I had reason to believe he might be violating the terms of his probation. He denied it. I told him I thought Ike was probably in trouble with police and asked him to promise not to hang out with him. He promised. And I said 'I mean a dead serious promise, not a fake promise.' And he swore he wouldn't hang out with Ike. But I think he was just saying it to get me off his back."

I took a bite of my biscuit, wondering if talking would do any good.

"So," he went on, "I called up a couple of investigators I know and asked if they knew anything about a guy named

Ike in that neck of the woods. And John, in the gang unit, said there's been some recent gang activity in the area with someone named Ike calling the shots. They don't think that's his real name. And John said he's recruiting new guys and sometimes threatens their families if the kids don't do as they're told. Which makes sense to me because I think Raymond really wants to succeed. I'm thinking he's being coerced."

"God, that's depressing."

"It is. And I asked if they knew of a store in the area with an Asian man behind the counter. They said there are a number of stores that fit that description."

"Well, what if we visit them today and see if I recognize the man?" I suggested.

He almost stared at me, but stopped himself before meeting my gaze, finishing off his last strip of bacon.

It took a while, but I finally convinced him it was a good idea. I mean, if we could find out which store it was, we might be able to prevent the armed robbery. So we drove around in his pickup, stopping at one store after another near Raymond's apartment. At the fourth store an Asian woman was behind the counter. And I stood a few feet back, trying to get a picture in my mind of the scene in my vision.

"Who works behind the counter at night?" I asked her.

"Husband."

"Do you have a picture of him?" I asked.

"He do nothing wrong," she said sharply.

"I know," I said. "We're trying to prevent an armed

robbery."

I knew that sounded strange but I thought just maybe she might be cooperative if she thought I was on her side. And it worked. After studying me for a moment, she pulled out her phone and showed me a picture of her husband and two grandsons with big smiles on their faces.

"Very handsome. All three of them," I said, and nodded at Brian.

"What time do you close?" he asked her.

"Eleven."

On the way back to my house I sensed Brian was hopeful he could somehow prevent the shooting. But now I was the one having doubts.

"If you're thinking of having extra patrols or hiring a security guard at the store, it might stop the shooting on that particular night," I said. "But if Raymond is being sucked into a gang, he probably won't survive for long."

"Exactly."

"So what do you have in mind?"

"Going after Ike. And talking with Raymond again."

Thinking about the danger Brian faced on a daily basis made me feel hollow inside.

"I'm not planning on staying in police work forever," he said, like he was reading my mind. "I graduate from law school in a year and a half."

"You're gonna be a lawyer?"

"Already talking with the D.A.'s office about a job."

"But that's a long time."

*

When we got to the house we fixed sandwiches and ate on the patio. Not looking at each other was so frustrating, though.

"I need a picture," I said. "Of your eyes."

"Yeah, me too. You have the most fabulous green eyes. Little sparkles of gold around the iris. I love your eyes."

Which made me blush.

"But," he said, "I fell for you the first time I saw you on stage, before I saw your eyes up close. And then, that night when we found you with a broken bottle in your hand at that low-class bar, ready to fight to the death, I said to myself: 'Self, this is one feisty, beautiful woman.'"

The memory made me laugh. I jumped up then to find my phone.

"All right," I said, "I need to take your picture."

"But…"

"Let's give it a try."

He looked down when I aimed my phone at him.

"Please?"

He relented, looking into the phone and I snapped several shots. Even though I could see his eyes through the lens, it didn't cause me to have a vision and we were both relieved. I examined the photos and found one that was perfect. In the picture I could see that his eyes were brown with green specks. And the photo made it look like he was gazing directly at me.

"My turn," he said, pulling his phone out of his pocket.

"But I need to put some lipstick…"

"Jenna, you don't realize how lovely you are. Now hold

still."

He took several pictures of me as I tried not to be self-conscious. Then I swallowed hard, realizing how much he meant to me.

"Wow," he said, scanning the photos. "I wonder, since you can look at me through a camera if maybe you can look at me in a mirror."

"Oh my God!" I squealed, grabbing his arm and pulling him with me through the kitchen and living room to the foyer where a gilt-framed mirror hung by the front door. "Okay, stand beside me."

But, instead, he stood behind me, holding onto my arms. And I knew why. Then he peeked around my head so he could look in the mirror and kissed my cheek without breaking eye contact. I pulled him closer to the mirror with me. It was heavenly. And I whirled around and focused on his handsome mouth and kissed him. He turned me away from him again, wrapping his arms around me from behind so we could use the mirror to swim in the depths of each other's eyes. What I saw was tenderness and yearning.

"We just need to install a mirror on the bedroom ceiling," he said, with a mischievous grin.

*

"You're looking like you feel better," Mrs. Robertson said, heading for my kitchen table.

She'd called saying she had more info on Eileen and wanted to stop by. I fixed us each a glass of ice water as she opened her laptop.

"Turns out Eileen was quite the entrepreneur," she said, rubbing her hands together. "She actually parlayed her psychic readings into a nice little business. She and her husband were able to buy a middle class home in town. She turned the parlor into a seeing room for her customers. Only did business during the daytime hours and only accepted male customers if they came with their wife or daughter. She protected her reputation that way, which was mighty smart. She and her husband were able to afford to send their son to college. Their daughter married a preacher. Pretty impressive, don't you think?"

"Wow."

"Indeedy," she said, beaming with pride. "I've never had so much fun researching a family history. Fascinating stuff. Anyway, I wanted to tell you in person that I was never able to find any significant medical issues in your father's family tree. He comes from middle class stock – doctors, businessmen, lawyers, homemakers. No witches. No fortune tellers. No pattern of early deaths."

"That's good to know," I said. "I appreciate all your hard work, Mrs. Robertson."

"I'll put together a written report for you with a list all the names, birth and death dates, places of birth and death, marriages, children, newspaper articles, obituaries, letters – everything I found. I'll mail you a nice fat envelope."

After showing her out, I tried to recall the vision I'd had with Meg. What had I actually seen when I looked into her eyes? I must've misinterpreted something about that scene in the hospital room. And then I nagged my dad about staying healthy and he ramped up his bike riding and that's what would get him killed!

I don't know why, but I was reminded of Superman, who despite being faster than a speeding bullet and all that stuff, could still get tripped up because he just couldn't be everywhere at the same time. And, of course, there was the Kryptonite. I imagined living the rest of my life trying to beat disease, accidents, shootings, abuse and all manner of bad things that happen to people, and failing! Being tripped up by my own Kryptonite.

"Shit!"

Even worse – I imagined never being able to look Brian in the eye. And I knew the novelty of gazing at each other in the mirror would wear thin. Who wants to be in love with a woman you can't look at? And that really pissed me off.

I returned to the kitchen, got a coffee mug from the cabinet and filled it with Chardonnay.

33.

By the time Brian returned I was good and drunk. And I mean good and drunk. I'd finished the white and was two thirds through the red and watching *Jane Eyre* on TV. He sat beside me, glanced at the screen, then leaned over and kissed my cheek.

"What's this?"

"*Jane Eyre*. It's a love story with lots of obstacles. But, unlike in real life, they eventually overcome all of them. Course, that includes a fire, a madwoman's death, wandering the moors and being rescued by a religious zealot – not exactly in that order."

"Rochester's an asshole."

"Rochester's not an asshole."

"Why is it so many women don't recognize an asshole when they see one?"

He picked up the remote and turned off the TV.

"Hey, what're you doing?" I cried.

"The question is: what're *you* doing? Looks like you're wasted."

"So?"

"So, are you supposed to mix alcohol with your pain meds?"

I closed my eyes and pursed my lips, trying to think of a witty comeback but, for some reason, I couldn't think of anything.

"I thought you'd like to know I talked again with Raymond and got the truth out of him," he said, his voice filled with irritation. "He admitted Ike and Stefon were threatening to hurt his mom if he didn't do as he was told."

Which sobered me up a bit.

"I told him while I understood his fear, that he should be more afraid of being sucked in by those guys," he went on. "He finally agreed to go with me over to headquarters and talk with an investigator in the gang unit. With any luck, Ike will be in a jail cell very soon."

And I began to cry. Which made me mad.

"Hey, this is good news," he said.

"I know, I know."

"Then, why…"

"Because I can't be a superhero." I staggered slightly as I rose, doing my best not to weave as I walked to the kitchen.

"A superhero?" he said, following me.

"And you'll get tired of me after a while, always avoiding your eyes. It'll get real old, real fast."

I was standing at the kitchen window when he caught

up with me and wrapped his arms around me from behind, putting his chin on my shoulder.

"I won't get tired of you," he whispered, kissing my cheek.

"Right!"

His kiss reminded me of what he said when we were at his house – "you're not alone anymore." And of how much I loved him.

I looked out on his garden, the garden he tended with such care, and wondered if it was possible I could do the same thing with my gift – mulch it, water it and prune it. I'd already proven I could steer my visions. Maybe I could fine-tune that skill. Maybe I could practice limiting how far into the future I saw. Like, just looking at what would happen in the next hour or the next day.

I leaned against him, but before I could speak, the doorbell chimed. He answered it and ushered Tia into the living room, holding three plastic containers. I started to introduce them.

"We've already met," she said.

She looked from him to me and back again, then scooted into the kitchen.

"I brought some homemade beef stew," she called out. "You can, like, freeze the containers and heat one at a time. Not that I made it, of course. My dad's the cook in the family. I'm popping them in your freezer."

And she was back in the living room in a flash.

"Just wanted to drop by and see how you're doing."

"I have to go to work now," Brian said. "You guys can

visit. Nice to see you again," he said to Tia and then kissed my forehead, giving me a quick hug. "I'll be over tomorrow."

Tia bugged her eyes at me as he closed the front door.

"Well, well," she said. "Here I was worried about you being lonely and all the time you..."

"He's the best thing that's ever happened to me. In fact, he's the love of my life."

I watched through the window as his truck pulled away and sighed.

"Well, if you don't mind my saying so, you don't look very happy about it," she said.

"I *am* happy about it," I said, but my voice wavered. "It's just that..."

And I crossed the room and got a tissue to blow my nose.

"Listen, I'm not gonna lie. Brian, like, called me and asked me to come over. He thought you needed a friend or something. But I have to confess I wasn't too thrilled, to be honest. Not sure he knows we're not exactly friends anymore."

"Oh, Tia. I've missed you so much."

I could feel her staring at me and I wanted so badly to look in her eyes and see the friend I'd known and loved for so long. It was obvious to me that the time had come to fix things between us.

"Well, what the hell's been going on these past few months?" she said.

I sat down on the sofa and patted the seat beside me.

"It's kind of hard to explain. But I'll try."

She sat down and stared at me, waiting. And before I lost my nerve, I looked directly into her big brown eyes.

I saw her crying in a hospital room, holding a woman's hand – it was me after my accident; then she was in a photo shoot, modeling a high fashion outfit; then she was arriving at an airport, a man walking beside her. I wanted to see more but forced myself to put the brakes on, using my internal crystal ball. I felt dizzy and weak as I came to, closing my eyes and grabbing a cushion for something to hold onto.

"Jenna, are you all right?"

I waved my hand at her.

"Did you just have a seizure or something?"

"Thank God, you're all right," I whispered.

"Thank God *I'm* all right?"

"Yes."

I leaned over and wrapped my arms around her.

"I've been so worried," I said.

I hugged her close. It was wonderful knowing her life had changed. And I thought about my visions. I was seeing a trajectory and that trajectory could be altered. Tia had stopped drinking and maybe it was my accident that did it.

"Why were you worried about me?" she asked. "I was worried about *you*! I don't get it."

"Oh it's such a long, complicated story."

"Just pretend you're tweeting and give me the short version."

"Okay. Here goes. When my mother died I inherited

her gift of clairvoyance, sort of. When I look into someone's eyes – someone I care about – I see their future."

I could feel her studying me like I was crazy. Which is
exactly what I expected all along.

"I think you might've succeeded in keeping it to tweet
length," she said. "But what the hell are you talking about?"

So I told her the whole story, beginning with what
happened with my mom in the hospital room, and everything I'd seen in my visions. And then I told her how I'd
seen Brian shot to death after a store robbery and everything we'd done since then to try to prevent it from happening. She never interrupted me. But skepticism oozed
from her pores.

"I've been afraid to tell anyone because I knew they
wouldn't believe me. I wouldn't have believed my mother if
she'd told me about it."

"When Brian said you needed to tell me something that
might be hard to swallow, it was, like, totally an under-
statement."

"Yeah."

"What did you see when you looked in my eyes?"

"The first time, right after Mom died, I saw you become
an alcoholic. And I saw you set your apartment on fire.
And I think your baby was inside."

I shook my head, trying to erase that disturbing image
from my mind.

"So that's why you told my dad I was an alcoholic."

"I didn't tell him you were an alcoholic. I just told him
there was a chance you might become one, you know,

since your mom had that kind of problem."

She grunted softly, obviously still steamed about it.

"But when I looked into your eyes just now, I saw a very different future. A good future. And I think something happened to change your trajectory."

"My trajectory."

She got up and paced around the living room, stopping to look at me and then pacing some more.

"This is too weird," she said.

"I know."

"I'm not sure about this… this… vision thing."

"Understandable."

She continued pacing, huffing and shaking her head as she walked. Then she stopped and stared at me, but I focused on her hands as they landed on her waist.

"God, Jenna, I hate it when you're right. I really hate it. I *was* drinking too much. And when you sicced my dad on me, he told me all about my mother and how her life and their marriage had been ruined. And then you got drunk and drove your damn car right through the wall into my dad's living room, nearly killing yourself and everyone in the house. And I was like, holy shit! But…"

"But you still don't believe me."

"I didn't say that."

"You didn't have to."

"Listen, let's go somewhere for dinner," she said. "You look like you could use a pu pu platter."

We went to our favorite cheap Chinese restaurant and she brought me up to date on her modeling jobs and the new guy she was dating and how her teaching job was going. And I told her about Brian. It was so nice to hang out with her again. I didn't realize how intensely I'd missed her. We still had work to do to repair our friendship but we'd taken the first step, thanks to Brian.

When we came out of the restaurant a soft rain was falling. We dashed to her car and headed back to my house. But when we turned onto my street the glow from the streetlight on the wet pavement seemed eerily familiar. And then it hit me.

"This is the night of the shooting," I said.

34.

"Pull over!" I cried.

"What shooting?"

"Remember, I told you I saw Brian shot to death after an armed robbery? Well, this is the same kind of misty rain. This is the night, I'm sure of it."

The distinct possibility that my vision might still come true made me weak. What if his talk with Raymond hadn't really worked? What if Raymond was just telling Brian what he wanted to hear? And what if Ike wasn't arrested anytime soon? And what if the two of them went to the store tonight anyway?

"Turn around," I said.

"I'm not driving to some crummy little store in a bad neighborhood where an armed robbery is going down. You think I'm crazy?"

"We have to."

"Forget it!"

"Tia! Please! Brian's life is at stake. Raymond's too."

"Who's Raymond?"

"I'll explain on the way. Just turn around."

"Jenna…"

"I'm begging you."

She shook her head and slapped the steering wheel with her hand.

"If I'd known being friends with you again might get me killed…" she sputtered, while executing a quick u-turn.

I guided her to Raymond's neighborhood, filling her in on Brian's "little brother" as we drove. I told her how Ike was threatening his mother and how Brian was trying to get Ike arrested.

"I don't like it," she said, turning left. "Not one bit. If those guys have guns, we have no business being here. You hear me?"

But I was studying the look of the wet pavement as light rain continued to fall. It looked just like my vision when Brian was chasing the man with the gun as he ran under the streetlight. I knew in my gut I was right.

"There's the store," I said.

Even in the dark, with the rain coming down, you could see the peeling blue paint and a sign above the door that was probably older than me. "Joe's Food & Liquor."

"Right here," I said, gesturing for her to park the car on the street.

"I'm not stopping. This is way too…"

"Fine, then. I'll jump." And I pulled the door handle.

"Jesus, Jenna!" she screamed, hitting the brakes.

She pulled to the curb a couple of car lengths beyond the store.

"Turn off the engine and lights," I said.

"You know this is, like, insane, right?" she said, making sure the doors were locked.

We sat in the dark, as the mist coated the car. Tia gripped the steering wheel and scanned our surroundings, repeatedly glancing in the rearview mirror and the side mirrors. I shifted around so I could look out the back, but the rear window was already covered by water droplets, and for a split second I had the feeling we were submerged in a lake. The store had a small neon sign that said "Lottery Tickets" and another one that said "Beer" and there were bars over the windows. The nearest working streetlights were a block away in either direction, making it much darker than I'd expected.

"What if they're already inside?" I whispered. "I'm going in."

"Jenna!"

But I was already out of the car. She jumped out too and followed me to the entrance, both of us looking nervously toward the street. I pushed the door open and we stepped inside.

The man behind the counter was the same one I'd seen in my vision, Mr. Song. I learned his name from his wife. He looked us over but said nothing. I grabbed Tia by the arm and pulled her to the back of the store.

"Jenna, what the hell are we doing?"

"Shh."

I gripped her arm and peeked around the shelves, waiting.

"What you need?" the owner called out, startling us.

"Uh, just choosing some drinks," I said.

We pretended to study the bottles of beer and wine but we were too nervous to speak. And a couple of minutes later the door opened and in walked Raymond and a tall, skinny guy who had to be Ike. The hairs on my arms prickled. Before I could decide what to do, we heard Ike mutter something and then Raymond pulled a gun, pointing it at Mr. Song.

"Raymond, is that you?" I heard myself call out as I moseyed to the front of the store as casually as possible. Tia whimpered but I sensed she wasn't following me.

Raymond jerked his head to the side and gave me a terrified look, still aiming his weapon at the store owner. Just as I reached the front, Mr. Song pulled a gun from his drawer and aimed it at Raymond's chest.

"Wait!" I cried. "Don't shoot." And I took a tiny step closer to Raymond. "Raymond, don't throw your life away. Put the gun down."

"I told you to check the fuckin' store first," Ike hissed as Raymond's eyes darted from Mr. Song to me.

I noticed Ike's hand move and I could hardly breathe, thinking of what was about to happen. Then I sensed movement behind the counter and I knew Mr. Song was about to pull the trigger. I threw myself at Raymond just as a loud crack of gunfire filled the small store. Tia screamed as Raymond and I tumbled to the floor. There was another gunshot as Mr. Song fired at Ike, who managed to escape as the bullet shattered the glass door. Raymond was trying to push me off of him, still gripping his weapon, but I hit his wrist as hard as I could and knocked it from his hand.

Then there was a siren outside and flashing blue lights.

"Oh my God!" I cried, struggling to get up.

"I use silent alarm. Police here!" Mr. Song shouted. "You stay down," he barked at Raymond. And he ordered me to kick the gun away.

But I was out the door. In the distance, I saw a police officer chasing Ike, both of them running like crazy, both of them with guns in their hands. I knew it was Brian even though I couldn't see his face. I took off after them through the drizzle, trying not to let them out of my sight, but they veered away from the street into the darkness. I struggled to keep up, but they were pulling away and I knew I was about to lose sight of them. My ribs were killing me but I couldn't slow down. I heard a police walkie-talkie up ahead, just like in my vision, and a siren behind me as a second cop car arrived at the store. Then I saw them running between two apartment buildings, a dim streetlight in the distance. This is where I'd seen Brian get killed!

"Nooo!" I shrieked at the top of my lungs.

And then Ike paused under the streetlight and aimed his weapon at Brian. There was a loud pop, pop. Brian was knocked backwards as though someone had punched him hard in the chest. But he extended his arm and returned fire before collapsing in the parking lot.

"Brian!" I screamed, racing toward him.

He was lying motionless on his side, his face pale and flaccid, his gun still in his hand when I reached him. I knelt down, burying my face in his shoulder and sobbed. Losing him was too cruel and I broke down completely there on the wet asphalt, wrapping my arms around him. My visions and warnings hadn't done any good. I wailed in grief.

But then he groaned softly and I lifted my head so I could see his face. I scanned his body for blood, but couldn't see any. He was soaked to the skin with rain and sweat, his hair plastered to his head. Then I noticed a deep furrow between his brows as he opened his eyes.

"Jenna?" he whispered.

Looking directly into his eyes, I was thrust immediately into a scene at the beach. The ocean was blue-green, the waves breaking as they rolled onto the sand. Brian and I were holding hands, walking barefoot in the surf. I looked up into his smiling eyes. And that's all I needed so I yanked myself out of the vision and back into the present.

"Oh, Brian…" I said, tears streaming down my face.

I hugged him gently, kissing his cheek.

"I'm wearing a bulletproof vest.

"I know."

"But you… you've got blood all over *you*."

When I looked down, there was a dark red stain on my top.

"It's not mine," I said.

Then two cops ran up, their weapons drawn. One of

them was on his two-way. The other spoke to Brian, his gun aimed across the parking lot.

"You wounded?"

"Bruised," Brian replied. "I'm wearing body armor."

The two officers moved carefully to the spot where Ike had fallen, their weapons aimed at his inert body. Then blue lights filled the misty night, as two police cars pulled up on the street behind us and another cop rushed toward us.

"EMT's on the way," he said.

The officers who had run after Ike called out then.

"He's dead."

"And Raymond?" Brian asked, looking from the officer to me, as it dawned on him whose blood was on my clothes.

I took my phone out of my pocket and texted Tia as an ambulance jumped the curb and rumbled in our direction. But she didn't reply.

"I need to find out what happened," I told him, kissing him as the paramedics prepared to load him into the ambulance. "I'll see you at the hospital."

One of the officers escorted me back to the store which had three cop cars and an ambulance parked out front, along with two TV trucks with satellite dishes on top. As we approached, two paramedics were lifting Raymond's stretcher into the vehicle. His shirt was gone and he was hooked up to an IV but that's all I could see. A woman officer was unrolling crime scene tape and wouldn't let me pass.

"But where's Tia?" I asked.

She gestured at a nearby police cruiser where I could see Tia in the back seat talking with an officer.

"Jenna!"

It was Alex Park walking toward me. Naturally, he was the reporter covering the shooting for his TV station.

"You involved in this?" he asked, noticing the blood on my shirt. He had this confused, surprised expression on his face.

I looked directly at him but only saw the dark eyes I used to find so attractive. Since there was no longer any emotional attachment, there was no vision.

"Alex," I said, suddenly wishing I could explain everything.

"Are you all right?"

"Yes, finally. But it took a long time."

Understanding showed in his face.

"I want you to know," I said, "that I'm sorry I hurt you. I never meant for any of that to happen."

"Don't worry about it."

"I do worry about it. You're a good guy. I hope you find someone who deserves you."

"Already have." His smile was genuinely warm and forgiving.

His cameraman was closing in on us, shooting video as he walked.

"See you around," I said and headed for the police car.

A tall black man in a suit intercepted me.

"I'm Investigator Washington," he said. "I'd like to ask

you some questions. I understand you intervened inside the store tonight."

"But what about Raymond? I asked.

"He's on his way to the hospital. Not sure how seriously he was wounded. Were you wounded too?" he asked, eyeing my top.

I looked down and noticed more blood than before.

35.

Sitting beside Tia in the back of the cop car, I realized the pain I thought was from my cracked ribs wasn't just coming from *inside* my chest. I pulled my top up to take a peek.

"Oh my God!" she cried.

"I think I was just grazed."

"Just grazed? You nearly got yourself killed! And you, like, saved that boy's life! Let me see."

And she proceeded to inspect me.

"I don't see a hole anywhere," she said. "But there's a lot of blood and you need to have a doctor look at that, like, right away."

"I will, I will."

Strange, I hadn't even felt it during all the chaos. I closed my eyes and leaned back.

"What about Brian?" she asked.

"He was wearing a bulletproof vest."

And she let out her breath as though she'd been holding it a long time. Then she reached over and took my hand in hers, but didn't say another word.

She drove me to the hospital after I convinced the detective I didn't need an ambulance. Once they confirmed the bullet had just grazed my belly and cleaned it up, Investigator Washington was waiting to question me. He was really curious about why Tia and I were at the store when the armed robbery went down. As much as possible I told him the truth. But I couldn't help wondering what Tia might've said.

"Well, you may know I've been dating Brian Mitchell."

"He told us."

"You may also know that Brian volunteers as a Big Brother. And Raymond – the guy who was shot in the store tonight – is one of his little brothers, so to speak."

"Mm-hm."

"So, Brian told me Raymond had gotten involved with a guy who might be pressuring him to join a gang and forcing him to prove himself by robbing a store."

"But that still doesn't explain why you and your friend were at *this* store on *this* particular night."

I paused, not sure what to say.

"I… I had a dream that something bad would happen tonight."

"But why did you decide Joe's Food and Liquor was the place?"

"It was the store closest to where Raymond lives," I said, hoping that was true. "And it just looked like the store in my dream."

Then he asked me to tell him what happened, start to finish, and I shared everything I could remember. Finally, he said I could go. I walked out into the ER waiting room to find Tia. But she wasn't alone. Her dad, my dad and Meg were pummeling her with questions. When they spotted me, Dad jumped up and wrapped his arms around me. Then Meg hugged me too.

"We were so worried," she said.

I avoided looking into their eyes but did my best to disguise what I was doing.

"Did Tia call you?" I asked, surprised they were here.

"No," Dad said. "Although it would've been nice if *someone* had called us. We were watching the news and, lo and behold, their lead story is an armed robbery where one of the robbers is killed, one is wounded and my daughter and her best friend just happen to be at the store when it all goes down!"

"That guy Alex – the one you introduced us to – he was the reporter," Meg said. "And he showed video of you and Tia!"

"That's how I found out too," Mr. Spencer said, giving Tia a look of fatherly irritation.

"What the hell were you two doing in such a dicey neighborhood?" Dad asked.

"Yeah!" said Mr. Spencer.

"It's a long story," I said. "And I'll tell you all about it, but first I need to find Brian." And I scanned the Emergency Room.

"Who's Brian?" Dad asked.

"I'll introduce you very soon." And I headed off, but turned around and walked backwards. "Oh, Dad, I've been meaning to tell you that too much bicycling isn't good for you. I read an article that says the number of fatal bike accidents is rising, mainly because drivers are careless and run over them."

"First you tell me to get healthy and now you're telling me not to ride my bike?"

I shrugged my shoulders and hurried off. I knew we'd have more conversations about it. And I'd have to think about whether to tell him about my visions.

I heard Tia informing everyone that Brian was my boyfriend as I approached the nurse's station.

"I'm looking for Brian Mitchell," I said. "He's the cop who was brought in here tonight."

A large nurse behind the desk looked at me like I was crazy and turned to a man standing beside me like I'd cut in line. So I pulled my phone from my pocket and texted him: "where r u?" There was an immediate reply: "Room 106."

I found him lying in bed with his sister by his side. Amy smiled warmly and hugged me.

"Thank you for nagging him to wear a bulletproof vest," she whispered.

Then I hurried to the other side of the bed and took his hand, very conscious of her presence. But it was obvious he didn't care who was in the room as he grabbed me and kissed my lips softly.

"I still haven't found out anything about Raymond," I

said.

"He's in emergency surgery right now to remove the bullet, but it looks like it missed his internal organs, thanks to you." Then he noticed my top. "But what the hell? You've got even more blood on you than before!"

"I was only grazed. I'm fine."

"Listen, I'll be in the waiting room," Amy said. "I can give you both a lift home when you're ready."

As soon as she was gone, Brian pulled me onto the bed with him so we were lying face to face, and wrapped his arms around me and kissed me.

"How did you know I was all right?" he asked. "I mean, when you found me."

"At first, I thought you were dead," I said, my voice cracking with emotion.

"It's all right," he whispered, stroking my hair.

"But when you came to, I looked in your eyes."

"And what did you see?"

"The two of us walking on the beach."

He hugged me tighter and we both said "ow." Which caused us to giggle.

And that's when a doctor in blue scrubs walked in, raising his eyebrows in amusement.

"I'm guessing this is not your sister," he said.

Brian laughed as I eased myself off the bed, trying to hide my blush.

"No, this is my bride-to-be, Jenna Stevens. Jenna, this is Dr. Kahn."

We nodded at each other.

"Okay," the doctor said, "I'm ordering you to stay home for ten days till that bruising gets better."

Brian took my hand like he wanted to keep me close. I couldn't take my eyes off him as he talked with the doctor about his prescription, about not lifting anything or doing anything strenuous, and coming in for a follow-up. I was still floating in that split second when he introduced me as his "bride-to-be." In all my romantic fantasies, I'd never once imagined the man I loved would ask me to marry him by announcing to an emergency room doctor that I was his fiancée. When we were alone again, he sat up gingerly, swung his legs over the side of the bed, took my hand again and kissed it.

"Jenna..." he said, but we were interrupted once more as the door burst open and in flooded everyone – Amy, Dad, Meg, Tia and Mr. Spencer.

"I made some new friends in the waiting room," Amy said, a big smile on her face.

"So this is Brian," Dad said, stepping forward to shake Brian's hand.

"This is my dad, Tom Stevens," I said. "And his wife, Meg."

She smiled and stood beside Dad.

"And this is Tia's father, Louis Spencer," I said.

"Nice to meet you," Mr. Spencer said, shaking Brian's hand as well. "Now, although I'm sure you're hoping we'll bend your ear for a while, I'm going to take Tia home now. Amy, very nice to meet you as well."

Meg took the hint and tugged on Dad's arm.

"We need to be going too," she said. "Amy says she can drive them home."

"Right," Dad said. "Look forward to seeing you again, Brian, when you're both rested."

And everyone disappeared except Amy who walked us to the ER entrance where she'd parked her car. We sat quietly in the back seat holding hands all the way to my house. I think she knew we were worn out because she didn't try to make conversation.

As soon as we were inside he took my hand and led me upstairs.

"You take the master bath and I'll shower in the other one," he said.

I thought about inviting him to join me but the idea seemed too forward or something. This was so different from being with Sam. A few minutes later, as I was toweling off, he knocked and then cracked the door slightly.

"Can I come in?"

"Just a second." And I threw on my little blue kimono. "Okay."

I didn't know what to expect but he'd wrapped a towel around his waist. He stood tentatively in the doorway as though waiting for permission to enter.

"Come over to the mirror," he finally said.

So we stood in front of the mirror looking at each other's reflections. He wrapped his arm around me and kissed the side of my face.

"First, I want to thank you for saving my life, and Raymond's life too. I'm amazed at how brave you were."

I swallowed hard, realizing then that my love for him had given me the strength I needed to use my strange gift – to force myself totally out of my comfort zone. Knowing I could lose him made the pain of the visions a small price to pay.

"Second, I want you to know I didn't mean to sound so presumptuous in the E.R.," he whispered. "It's just that, in that split second before I introduced you to the doctor, I thought 'girlfriend' didn't hold a candle to how I feel about you and what you mean to me and how I want to spend the rest of eternity with you. So I couldn't bring myself to call you my girlfriend. It was completely inadequate. Because I love you with every heartbeat, every breath, every cell in my body."

I opened my mouth to speak but he wasn't through.

"You *will* marry me, won't you?" he asked, a hopeful, uncertain expression suddenly crossing his face.

"Oh, Brian," I said, leaning my head on his shoulder.

"Say yes," he whispered.

"But…"

"There's a but?"

"When I thought I'd lost you tonight, I…"

My heart was in my throat and I couldn't continue.

"Shh. When the investigation is over and I'm cleared for duty, I've asked for a desk job. And law school graduation will be here before you know it."

So I whispered "yes" and spun around so I could hold his warm body in my arms. It felt so good, I didn't want to let go.

"There's one last thing before we get some sleep," he said, taking my hand and leading me into the bedroom. "I want you to take off that pathetic excuse for a robe." He untied it and pushed it from my shoulders, then dropped his towel. "And, if you don't mind, I very much want your naked body next to mine."

And we climbed carefully into bed and made love with the most exquisite gentleness before falling asleep in each other's arms.

36.

We waited until the third Saturday in October. I was in my bra and panties and Brian's favorite tiny kimono, fixing my hair at the bathroom vanity when he stepped from the shower. I smiled at him in the mirror, admiring his beauty, but he quickly wrapped the towel around his waist.

"No peeking," he teased, stepping close behind me and kissing me on the neck as his hands came to rest on my waist. "You nervous?"

I chuckled, but before I could reply, there was a tingling in my arms and fingers and a tiny flash of light somewhere in my brain. I closed my eyes and grunted softly.

"What?" he asked.

"Something's going to happen."

"What do you mean?"

"I feel it. Something's going to happen today."

"Damn right, we're getting married today!"

He kissed my cheek, gazing into my eyes in the mirror.

"Something else," I said. "This is the first premonition I've had since…"

"You have premonitions in addition to visions?"

"Well, they're not premonitions exactly. Just feelings that something's about to happen. I never know what it is ahead of time."

"One thing's for sure, our life together won't be boring." And he grinned.

That's when the doorbell rang. It was only a little after 11:30 and the ceremony wasn't until 2:00.

"I'll get it," I said. "You can slip into something a little less comfortable."

"Well, if it isn't the bride-to-be, herself," Tia gushed when I opened the door.

She bustled in like she was in charge, lugging two potted pink azaleas.

"What're you doing here so early?" I asked.

"Someone had to decorate," she said, setting the pots down on the coffee table. "You guys go about your business. Don't mind me. I'm, like, bringing more stuff in."

"I hope you didn't get carried away. It's just supposed to be a quiet affair."

"Go beautify yourself!" she called over her shoulder as she headed out to her car.

I shook my head, smiling as I trotted back upstairs. An hour later, Brian and I ventured downstairs in jeans to get a sandwich and I couldn't believe how she'd transformed the living room. She'd pushed the sofa and the coffee table to the wall for more floor space, placing white folding chairs in neat rows for the guests. At the front of the room was a wedding arch draped in sheer white chiffon with white and pink silk flowers across the top. Half a dozen pink azaleas with gauzy pale pink bows transformed the room into a pretty garden. She had draped the hutch with a white tablecloth and placed three floating candles with pink flowers as a centerpiece. Plates and silverware were arranged on the left with a space at the other end for the wedding cake. The kitchen table was also covered with a white tablecloth with champagne flutes and drink napkins arranged just so.

"Wow," said Brian.

"You like it?" she asked, practically bouncing on her toes.

"It's positively enchanting," I said, admiring the effect. "It looks like springtime flowers in a field of green and blue."

"And the champagne's already chilling," she said, opening a blue cooler on the floor by the kitchen table to reveal a dozen bottles. "Oh, and I bought sparkling white grape juice for Meg, Daisy, Raymond and anyone else who doesn't want to imbibe." And she pointed to the fridge. "Amy and your mom are bringing Daisy," she continued, looking at Brian. "Your police chaplain buddy is bringing Raymond." Then she looked at me. "And your dad and Meg are picking up the cake!"

"Thank you, Tia," I said. "You've outdone yourself."

She heaved a happy sigh as she surveyed her handiwork.

At precisely two o'clock, she tapped on the bedroom door and pushed it open.

"Oh! My! God!" she said, her brown eyes even bigger than usual.

I'd chosen a tea length white wedding gown that flared slightly at the hem with an overlay of sheer white lace on the bodice. My hair was off my face in a loose chignon, with tiny white silk flowers in the back.

"You look gorgeous," she whispered.

"You do too."

Her pale aqua dress had a mandarin collar and cap sleeves and she looked like she should be on the cover of *Glamour* magazine.

"I think I'm gonna cry," she said, handing me my bridal bouquet. "Now, your dad will meet you at the bottom of the stairs. Don't come down till you hear the music, okay? I've already taken Brian down and put him in his place. Ha ha – put him in his place. Get it?"

And she was gone.

As I waited for my cue I thought about my mother, wishing she were here on my wedding day. I wanted to tell her that she didn't really have to live a lonely life, that she didn't have to avoid being close to people. I wanted to tell her that you didn't have to disengage to avoid the pain because the pain is worth it. After all, life itself is a big risk. Nothing is guaranteed. Of course, I couldn't change the past, but maybe I could help shape the future. And while I knew there were still big challenges ahead, I had Brian now. And that made me so happy, I had to blot the tears welling in the corners of my eyes.

That's when I heard the first strains of *Here Comes the Bride.* It was a guitar version and I realized as I started down the stairs that it wasn't a recording.

I felt like a butterfly floating down the stairs after shedding my chrysalis and spreading my wings. Dad was waiting for me at the bottom with an emotional smile on his face. He looked debonair in a dark grey suit and blue tie. I took his arm and we walked together to the front of the room where Brian was waiting in a black tuxedo, looking for all the world like a handsome prince waiting for Cinderella. His eyes sparkled with mischief and I dared not look into them.

Maria was the one playing the guitar, standing on the opposite side of the room in a pale yellow dress with her long black hair on her shoulders. She flashed a warm smile at me, making me very glad we'd renewed our friendship even though we didn't spend our days together in the classroom anymore.

I glanced at the guests and noticed Daisy wearing the pretty pink dress I'd given her. Her mom had been reluctant to let me be her "big sister" at first, but seemed to be getting used to the idea. When I was ordered to do community service for my DUI, becoming a big sister for Daisy was the first thing that popped into my head.

Raymond looked sharp in the blue suit Brian bought especially for the occasion. He was still recuperating but would graduate with his class in the spring. Brian was helping him with college applications. Thank goodness Mr. Song agreed not to file charges after Brian explained how Raymond was being pressured.

Dad kissed my cheek as he deposited me next to Brian, who reached down and took my right hand. Tia appeared on my left, taking the bouquet, and she and Dad sat down next to Meg and my grandparents.

The ceremony was short and sweet, with the chaplain making some lovely remarks about marriage and commitment and then we each said the brief vows we'd written, Brian first.

"First, I promise to love you forever, no ifs, ands or buts. Second, I promise to be your partner facing whatever life has in store for us. Third, in addition to being madly in love with you, I promise to be your best friend and to always be there for you like you've already proven you'll be there for me. I just hope I can live up to your example of compassion for others. And fourth, I want you to know that from the first time I looked in your eyes, I knew in my gut that you were my soul mate."

His voice quivered slightly and he gave my hand a squeeze, but he was gazing at my mouth, not my eyes.

I swallowed nervously, trying to steady my voice as I focused on his wonderfully expressive eyebrows.

"I promise to help you with the garden, and to eat your produce, which is heavenly."

That made him smile.

"And," I continued, "I'm so thankful I found you sitting on my front porch that day and that you cared enough to track me down. A part of me is stunned that I'm the one who gets to marry you – you are *that* special. You're the love of my life and I shall hold you in my heart until the end of time."

I knew it wasn't time yet but I leaned forward anyway and gave him a kiss and then nodded at the chaplain who proceeded to ask us whether we each took the other as husband and wife, and promised to cherish each other through sickness and health, and we both said "I do."

I tried to look in his eyes then, as he leaned down to kiss me, but he closed them.

"I love you," he whispered.

"God, I love you too."

There was a round of applause and I took his arm as we turned to greet our family and friends as husband and wife. The first person I saw was Meg, whose belly seemed much larger than the last time I'd seen her. She was wearing a light green dress. She and Dad stepped forward and Meg gave me a hug as Dad shook Brian's hand. When she stepped back her mouth opened, but then it twisted into a grimace and she looked from me to Dad.

"Tom..." she said.

But Dad was laughing and welcoming Brian to the family.

"Tom!"

"Yes, honey?"

"My water just broke."

"Your... but... but you're not due yet," Dad sputtered.

I looked down and sure enough, her shoes and the

carpet were wet.

"No cause for alarm," Amy said, stepping forward to stand next to Meg. "It's not uncommon for the amniotic sac to rupture as you go into labor. Tom, you just need to call the O.B. and have her meet you at the hospital. The baby will be just fine. Brian, can you get some towels? Jenna, bring some plastic garbage bags to protect the upholstery in the car."

Dad called the obstetrician, Brian dashed upstairs for the towels and I hurried to the kitchen for the garbage bags, thankful Amy was calmly telling us all what to do.

"I'll ride with you and Tom to the hospital," Amy said, and Meg seemed relieved to have a doctor-in-training accompany them.

And then they were out the door, with Dad and Amy on either side of Meg – Dad carrying the towels and Amy carrying the plastic bags – and both of them holding Meg's arms.

"Is she gonna have the baby now?" Daisy asked me.

"I think so," I answered, giving her a hug.

37.

Needless to say, the little wedding reception was even smaller and shorter than we planned. We did have a piece of wedding cake and everyone toasted our happiness with champagne or faux champagne. Afterwards, Brian and I ran upstairs to change.

"Wow," he said as soon as we were alone. "You were right. Something else did happen."

"I'm just glad it's something good."

"Before we go I have a wedding gift for you," he said, pulling a large box from the closet and setting it on the bed.

I ripped the silver wrapping paper off and opened it to find a real crystal ball on a wooden stand. I laughed out loud and gave him a peck on the lips. Together, we pulled it out and set it on the dresser.

"It's milky quartz," he said.

"It's perfect." And I rubbed my hand over the smooth

globe. "Thank you." And I kissed him again and hugged him tight.

"You've still got flowers in your hair," he said.

He helped me remove them and I pulled my hair down on my shoulders as he watched me in the mirror.

"My soul mate," he whispered.

"The love of my life," I whispered back, and we wrapped our arms around each other as we gazed into each other's eyes in the mirror. "You remember when you told me you had a gift too – that you could look into people's eyes and see their futures? Remember that?"

"Yeah," he said.

"Well, I think you do have a gift, at least when it comes to me. It's uncanny, really, how many times you've read my mind, answering questions I never asked."

"That's because I'm so tuned into you. It's like that song: *If you're a rose, then I'm your garden.*"

He kissed me and held me close and I wished for a moment that we didn't have to rush off. But we had to postpone any more lovey-dovey stuff so we could head to the hospital.

Of course, he drove. I didn't have a car and my license had been revoked for six months. But I was getting used to using transit. I'd studied the schedule and figured out how to take the train for my upcoming audition at the Northside Playhouse. And I figured I could also ride the train to and from rehearsals and shows – if I got the part. Just like they did in New York City.

Interestingly, Randall's threats about my never getting

another acting job in Atlanta hadn't panned out the way he predicted. Some of my acting buds told me *he* was having a hard time getting roles now and that his reputation took a hit when his wife made all kinds of accusations when she filed for divorce.

We sat in the waiting room for a couple of hours, which gave me time to think. What I saw in my visions was like a flight path, but that path could be shifted. So it was possible I could alter my dad's trajectory just like I accidentally changed Wendy's life when I blabbed about Randall cheating on her. And like I helped change the future for Brian, Raymond and Tia. I also realized my visions weren't necessarily the whole story and I might misinterpret what I saw. But at least I no longer viewed life as a river that gravity forced over a precipice. There were no Fates spinning our destinies with a thread of life – nothing is necessarily inevitable, except for death.

We dozed off sometime after midnight with Brian sprawled across three chairs, his head in my lap. I was awakened when my phone buzzed.

"Your baby brother has arrived," Dad said.

I poked Brian to wake him up. It was a little after two in the morning.

"Can we see him?" I asked.

"Come on up," Dad said, his voice a mixture of elation and exhaustion.

The room was lit only by a lamp on the nightstand. Dad was still in his dress slacks and white shirt, with his rumpled sleeves rolled up to his elbows, but the tie and jacket were long gone. He was seated in a chair he'd dragged to the bedside so he could be close to Meg. And there in her arms, wrapped in a blue and green striped blanket, was the tiny baby. We could just see the crown of his fuzzy head.

Meg smiled up at us and pulled the blanket back slightly so we could see his face. He had round pink cheeks and an angelic expression. He was sound asleep.

"Beautiful," I whispered.

"Handsome," Brian corrected me.

"He's perfect," said Dad dreamily and Meg smiled.

"Wanna hold him?" she asked me.

"Of course." Although I was a little uncertain.

Dad jumped up from his chair and gestured for me to sit. Then Meg carefully placed their little bundle of joy in my arms. He made a tiny little noise and crinkled his nose.

"Welcome, brother-in-law," Brian said softly, leaning over my shoulder, and we all laughed quietly.

"What's his name?" I asked.

"Ethan Brett Stevens," Dad replied.

"Ethan," I said, trying it out. "I like it."

And that's when my brand new baby brother opened his sweet blue eyes and, without thinking, I looked straight into them. Through his eyes, I saw his mother's face as she held him in her arms, and then he was swinging in the back yard and then... I clamped my eyes shut and forced myself to pull out of the vision. Brian must've sensed what was happening because when I opened my eyes again, he was squatting beside me, holding the baby with me, his big hand under little Ethan's head.

"He looks strong and healthy," he said. "Congratulations to you both."

"Thank you," Meg said, holding her arms out to reclaim her newborn son.

Brian helped make the transfer and when we stood to go he held my waist tightly, making sure I was steady.

"You flying out tomorrow?" Dad asked.

"Later this morning, actually," Brian said.

"I've never been to Cozumel but I've seen pictures and I know it'll be a wonderful honeymoon," Meg said.

Dad hugged me and Brian as we left the room, all of us turning the page on a new chapter in our lives.

I told Brian what I'd seen in Ethan's eyes on our way home. But I didn't tell him how alarmed I suddenly felt about having a child of our own. Holding the baby made me realize how hard it would be to have a child whose eyes you constantly avoided. And then there was the fear of passing along my gift. But I decided not to think about all of that right now. Right now I wanted to immerse myself in the happiness of my new life.

*

"Is this the scene you saw of us walking on the beach?" he asked.

We were barefoot in the shallow surf, the white sand sparkling in the morning sun.

"No, that vision was way in the future."

"How do you know?"

"Your hair was grey and you had wrinkles."

We both laughed.

"So… how do I look when I'm old?" he asked.

"Like a sexy, brown-eyed, old fart."

And he smiled big time, grabbed me up and swung me around.

The End

Review it
Thank you for reading *VisionSight*. If you enjoyed it,
please help spread the word by posting a brief customer
review wherever you buy books. Or recommend it to your
friends, in person or on social media. Maybe tell your
favorite bookstore or book club. Thanks so much!

If you liked *VisionSight* you might also enjoy...
The Time Telephone by Connie Lacy

What if you could save your mother's life by calling her in
the past on a time telephone?

17-year-old Megan McConnell is grieving, bitter and
skeptical after her mom is killed covering the war in
Afghanistan. When she stumbles on an antique phone in
the farmhouse where her mother grew up, she decides she
has nothing to lose, and maybe everything to gain by
giving it a try. She's also desperately hoping for another
chance at a real mother-daughter relationship with a
woman who chose her career as a foreign correspondent
over motherhood.

With encouragement from a couple of unlikely friends,
including a boy who's in love with her, Megan speaks with
her mom in the past.

The Time Telephone is an intriguing coming of age story
about a teenager dealing with feelings of rejection and
abandonment.

About the author

Connie Lacy writes speculative fiction, magical realism and historical fiction, all with a dollop of romance. She worked for many years in radio news as a reporter and news anchor. She and her husband live in Atlanta.

Sign up for occasional updates

www.ConnieLacy.com

I'd love to hear from you

Email: connielacy@connielacy.com
Website: www.ConnieLacy.com
Facebook: www.Facebook.com/ConnieLacyBooks
Twitter: https://twitter.com/cdlacy
Goodreads: www.Goodreads.com/ConnieLacy
Instagram: www.instagram.com/connielacy_author
Pinterest: www.pinterest.com/cdlacy0736

Acknowledgements

Special thanks to Jennifer Perry and Doug Lacy for their valuable feedback and suggestions.

"If You're a Rose" lyrics ©2015 by Kyle Lacy. Used with permission. www.kylelacymusic.com